D, MY NAME IS
Danita

Look for these other books about best friends
by NORMA FOX MAZER:

A, My Name Is Ami

B, My Name Is Bunny

C, My Name Is Cal

E, My Name Is Emily

D, MY NAME IS
Danita

NORMA FOX MAZER

AN
APPLE
PAPERBACK

SCHOLASTIC INC.
New York Toronto London Auckland Sydney

"To Arnold With Whom I Used to Pick Raspberries When We Were Children Thirty-Five Years Ago" by Hilda Mader Wilcox. Reprinted by permission of the author.

ISBN 0-590-43656-2

12 11 10 9 8 7 6 5 4 3 2 1   8   4 5 6 7 8 9/9

Printed in the U.S.A.   40

*For my sister Linda —
love, friendship, Thysania zenobia and
"Mega excellent dude!"*

D, MY NAME IS
Danita

Chapter 1

When I was born I weighed less than a pound. "Not even as much as a loaf of bread," my mother always says. When my parents, who are Jody and Daniel Merritt, finally took me home from the hospital, I was four months old, and I still didn't weigh as much as some babies do at birth.

"You were smaller than my thumb," my dad says. "And you're still a tiny thing."

Well, maybe . . . but now I'm nearly fourteen, and I want my parents to stop fretting about me. I want them to stop hovering over me as if I'm a delicate plant that someone in the big, bad world is going to step on and crush.

Here's the way it goes in our house. In the morning, as soon as I enter the kitchen, my mother says, "How did you sleep, Danita?" My father hands me my vitamins and says, "Kiddo, did you brush your teeth good?" And even my little sister gets into the act. "Dani, were you cold last night? Did you have enough blankets?"

I swallow vitamins and say, "Warm as toast, slept fine, and *always* brush my teeth." Which, just then, are showing in what's meant to pass for a smile. Finally, we move on to other things.

My father begins reading out loud a letter someone wrote to the newspaper. " 'Dear Editor, we women do not appreciate the hairy apes that are called men today.' "

"Hairy apes!" Lizbeth shrieks.

Dad smiles. For years he's been collecting the dumbest letters people write to the newspaper. He says someday he'll make a book of them and call it *Stupid Opinions*. He'll print it right at his shop. " 'How can any self-respecting man cover his face with a hairy mess called *beard*?' " he goes on. " 'Did you ever see one of these ape-men eat?' " He's laughing too hard to continue. "How do you guys vote on this one?"

"Definitely a saver, Dad," I say. Ooops. Why did I say anything? Now he's got me on his mind again.

He fixes his eyes on me and says, "That's not the way you plan to go to school, is it, sweetie?"

Certainly, it is. I'm wearing sneakers, white ankle socks, mauve pants turned up at the ankles, and a mauve-and-white diagonally striped sweater. Plus, my best silver double hoop earrings. I spent a lot of time last night and again

4

this morning figuring out what I was going to wear.

"Pretty outfit, Dani, but it's raining."

"Dad," I plead, "it's only dripping." It's a soft rain, and I look forward to walking in it. I might put on a jacket, but not a raincoat! Not rubbers! Not an *umbrella*.

"I don't want you taking a chance of catching a cold."

"Which could turn into flu which could turn into pneumonia which could cause me to die at a young, tender age," I say.

"Very funny," Mom says. "I want to see that raincoat walking out the door this morning, Dani."

"Lizbeth — " I begin. I don't even know what I'm going to say about Lizbeth. Just something about them never bugging her. But Mom reads me on that, too.

"Sweetie, you've had every little horrible virus and nasty bug in the world. Lizbeth has never been ill a day in her life. She's healthy as a horse."

The perfect thing to say about my sister! She's a horse fanatic. She sleeps, eats, talks, thinks, and even *wears* horses. This morning she's got a wooden horse on a chain around her neck, a T-shirt with an embroidered red horse on the pocket, and a belt around her jeans with a brass horse-head buckle. I think her secret desire is to *be* a horse.

I gulp milk, grab a piece of toast. " 'To Arnold

with whom I used to pick raspberries when we were children thirty-five years ago,' " I whisper under my breath, trying to ignore my family. That's the title and also the beginning line of the poem I'm going to recite for Greasepaint tryouts. It's a very sad poem, about someone who killed himself a long time ago. Every time I recite it all the way through, I cry.

"See you guys," I say, putting down the glass.

"Hold it." Dad takes my arm. "In case you haven't noticed, sweetie, breakfast is on the table."

"Dad, I have to get to school early."

There's less than a week until tryouts. I'm definitely not an actress; just the opposite, in fact! But somehow I've got it into my head that this year I *have* to be in drama society. Which means I need every bit of practice I can get before tryouts. And not in my bedroom, where I feel safe, but on the spot (so to speak), on the stage, in the auditorium, facing those rows and rows of seats, where I feel . . . I won't lie to you . . . *terrified*.

Mom slides a plate of loose, whitish scrambled eggs in front of me. Dad muscles me (gently, I admit, but still muscles me) into a chair. "Get any skinnier and you'll blow away in the first stiff wind."

I choke back a yell of outrage. If I blow my cork, they'll say I'm not acting like myself and conclude I'm getting sick and may not even let me go to school. According to my parents, I'm "myself" when I'm happy, calm, and cheerful.

6

But then who am I when I'm feeling ugly, irritable, and disagreeable? I swallow a forkful of slimy egg, trying not to see it or taste it.

By the time I get to school, it's much too late to go to the auditorium to practice. "Disaster day," I mutter between my teeth and slam my locker door a few times. Fortunately, I finally notice the note on the floor that Laredo slipped into the locker.

DANI, LUNCH MUNCHIES TOGETHER PER UZUAL?? GUESS WHAT! I SAW YOUKNOWWHO ON THE WAY TO SCHOOL. LOVE YA. W.W.

W.W. stands for Wild Woman. Youknowwho is Jon Haberle, a senior-high boy I have a crush on.

Chapter 2

Laredo and her mom live on the east side of the city on Park Street in an apartment, which happens to be in the same building and above a place called the People's Beer Hall. The first time Laredo invited me for a sleepover, Mom and Dad drove me there together. They parked the car, got out, looked up and down the street like a pair of housing inspectors, and advanced with murmurs and frowns on the People's Beer Hall.

"Your friend lives *here*?"

"Not in there, Mom and Dad. Upstairs!"

Laredo's door is next to the bar, but completely separate. You go up a long, narrow flight of stairs. The apartment is at the top. Up we went, a parent in front of me, a parent in back of me.

"You could get a buzz on from just breathing the smell off these walls," Dad said.

I prayed he wouldn't say anything like that in front of Laredo's mom. She was already going to be late for work, just so she could be interviewed by my parents. I should have prayed harder! Dad asked a million questions.

"What time will you be home from work, Mrs. Gerardi? What are Laredo's rules for being alone? Will you be calling the girls from work to check that they're okay?"

Finally he and Mom ran out of questions and agreed with Mrs. Gerardi that Laredo and I were responsible people and could take care of ourselves for a few hours.

"Well, that wasn't so bad," Laredo said, after they all left. She locked the door.

"Oh, no? Did you happen to notice that my father thinks I can't walk and chew gum at the same time?"

"Dani, don't complain; it's adorable the way your father worries over you." She went into the kitchen and plugged in the popcorn maker. "I decided tonight that he's Mr. Ideal Dad. He's a ten, Dani."

"If you say so."

"Plus, he and your mom are still a big romance item. Another ten!"

Laredo was impressed that every year my parents celebrated two anniversaries, the day they got married and the day they met.

"Plus, they've been married *sixteen* years." She poured in a cup of popcorn. "My parents

9

couldn't even hold it together for three crummy years. And, your father likes me."

"Why should he get credit for that, Laredo?"

"Let me put it to you this way. Does *my* father like you?"

"Laredo, he lives three thousand miles away in Texas. He wouldn't know me if he fell over me."

"My point exactly. Your father is here, on the spot, present and accounted for. And I'll tell you something else about your father."

"I know you will," I said over the noise of popping corn. "You're on a roll."

"He thinks *you* are the greatest thing that ever happened to him, Dani. And he tells you so. The last time my father told me anything, I can't even remember."

"I'm sure he loves you," I said.

"Yeah, he has a great way of showing it." She dumped the melted butter into the popcorn and we went into the living room to watch TV.

Laredo and I met for the first time last year in gym, on the volleyball court. She was new in school. I noticed her right away — tall, lanky, all this hair flying wildly around her head. Very beautiful, and she looked athletic. Ha! She was all thumbs and clumsy feet. She did things like bumping the ball backward instead of over the net, losing us the point. Not once, not twice, but three times!

"What a spaz that new girl is," Heidi Gretz said, not even bothering to lower her voice.

I glanced at Laredo. I thought she'd be

crushed. Instead, she was laughing. "Sorry, guys, I'm a total flake on a court. Keep the ball away from me!"

Later, I asked her to come home with me after school. I liked her — there was something so different about her. One thing was her enthusiasm for everything. "This is *great*," she said the moment we walked into my house. "I love this place! Oh, look, a breakfast nook! Your father made this? I've never had a breakfast nook." She ran from room to room, looking at everything. "A family room! Your dad built that fireplace? I don't believe it! And you have *two bathrooms.*"

Laredo had lived in apartments all her life. "Eight, no, *ten* apartments, counting the two I don't remember from when I was a baby."

"It must be fun living in different places. I've always lived in this same boring house."

"Oh, ta! Poor baby!" "Ta!" was Laredo's expression of sympathy, scorn, warmth, irony, whatever. "Ta!" was for everything, and I picked it up from her. We said "ta" to each other when we met, and "ta" when we parted. It became our special word.

One day we made ourselves blood sisters. Laredo's idea, of course. She sterilized a needle over the kitchen stove. I'm sure I turned pale. I closed my eyes and tried to make a joke. "Practicing to be a doctor?" Laredo wanted to go to medical school someday.

"It'll be fast," she said, and a moment later, "Okay, open your peepers."

11

I saw a thin line of red dots. Quickly, she pricked her thumb and put it over mine. Our blood mingled.

"Ta, Dani," she said solemnly. "We're linked forever."

Chapter 3

Laredo gave me an elbow in the ribs and rolled her eyes at a boy walking by us. "Oh, my soul," she sighed. She craned her neck after him.

We were sitting on the bench near the fountain in the Springfield Mall after school. We'd come over so Laredo could look at guys and I could look at Jon Haberle. He worked at Ice Dreams, and from where we were sitting I could see him in his little white-walled space. I'd like to say I could see him clearly, but since I'm nearsighted, this wasn't the case.

"Don't you think Jon looks like — " I mentioned a movie star.

Laredo looked dubious. "Maybe."

I drifted off into one of my daydreams about Jon noticing me. It could happen here . . . or in school. . . . He'd come up to me, stop, *really look at me*, and then he'd take my hand, gaze straight into my face and say, *Danita, I've wanted to talk to you for so long . . . all I think about is you.* "Ohhh," I sighed.

"What?" Laredo said.

"Nothing. Just . . . Jon."

"You could make something happen with him, you know, Dani. You could go over there and order something and — "

"No, I couldn't!"

" — and then you'd talk to him, and — "

"I *can't*, Laredo."

"Why not? I'd do it."

"I'm not you. And my father says there's no use trying to be something you're not."

"With all respect to your father, that's not convincing."

I tried to think of a better reason why I couldn't talk to Jon. "He's a *junior*."

"So?"

"Laredo, junior boys are not interested in eighth-grade girls."

"Dani, you know what I think? Boys are just like everybody else — insecure. I bet they love it if a girl does some of the work for them. Maybe Jon is shy, too."

"You think so?"

"Why not? You'll never know, though, if all you do is *lurk*."

I watched Jon dipping ice cream. I admired the serious way he bent over and scooped, then

14

flashed his gorgeous smile when he held the cone out to the customer.

Laredo tapped my arm. "Cute-boy alert. Over by Kroll Book Store. Put on your glasses."

The boy Laredo had noticed was leaning against the wall outside the store, one foot back up behind him. Even with my glasses, I couldn't see him that well, except that he was older.

"He's giving us the big once-over," Laredo said. She stood up. "I'm going to go over there and stare back at him."

"Laredo!" I grabbed her shirt. "You can't do that."

"Yes, I can."

Before she could move, the boy moved first. He strolled down the aisle. He was coming toward us. Laredo sat down again with a smile. "He's adorable," she said. "Hey, cutie . . . love your ponytail . . . look this way . . . I desire you," she crooned softly. But as he got closer, she shut up.

He was definitely staring at us. Embarrassed, I pulled off my glasses and looked down. As he passed, all I saw were his feet. Red sneakers. Bare ankles. No socks. Then he disappeared around a corner.

My sister came into my room that night while I was doing homework and said she wanted to talk to me. "Sure. Go ahead."

"I want you to *listen*." Lizbeth was wearing her nightgown. She had her toothbrush in her hand. "Close your book. Sit up."

I snapped my book shut and sat up on my bed, crossing my legs. "Is this posture satisfactory, your highness?"

"That's good."

She never gets it when you're being sarcastic.

She fiddled with her toothbrush. I don't know how she'd managed, but she'd found one with a horse on it. "You know, Dani," she said, "we women have to be prepared for anything."

I could have laughed, I guess. "What TV show did you pick that up from?" I said. "On second thought, I don't want to know." I opened my book and started studying again.

"Dani!"

"What?"

"I want to ask you something. Can I come to you for advice?"

I turned the page. "What's the matter, what kind of advice?"

"Nothing now. I just wanted to know for the future if I could. Because sometimes I think of things — and, you know, I get sort of worried."

"The same thing happens to me, Lizbeth." I put my finger in my place. "I think of things and I get worried."

"You do?"

"Definitely."

"I thought nothing worried you, Dani!"

"Lizbeth. Everybody worries about stuff.

Didn't you ever hear Daddy worrying about things? Everybody worries!"

"I'm glad you told me."

She was looking at me seriously. It was intense, a real moment. For once, I felt very close to her.

Chapter 4

"My poem is called, 'To Arnold With Whom I Used To Pick Raspberries When We Were Children Thirty-five Years Ago,' " I said.

"A bit louder, please." Mrs. Avora, sitting below the stage in the first row, tossed her purple scarf over her shoulder.

"My poem is called, 'To Arnold With Whom I Used To Pick Raspberries When We Were Children Thirty-five Years Ago,' " I repeated loudly.

"Is that the title, the whole thing?" Mrs. Avora asked.

"Yes." Why had I picked a poem with such a long title? My hands started sweating. "It's by a poet called Hilda Wilcox."

I looked at Laredo, who was sitting in the second row, to see how I was doing. I should have worn my glasses. Laredo's face was a blur.

But I could see that she was jabbing a finger toward her mouth. We'd agreed on that signal if I wasn't speaking loudly enough.

"IT'S BY A POET CALLED HILDA WILCOX," I almost shouted.

"Danita, are you planning to repeat everything?" Mrs. Avora touched her hair. It was cut straight across her forehead. "I surely hope not."

"This poem is not what you usually think a poem is. It doesn't rhyme and it's not boring." I took a deep breath. Was I speaking clearly? I had a tendency to mumble in public. I had to remember to speak slowly and distinctly. "It's sad," I said, emphasizing each word. "It's about two people — "

"Danita," Mrs. Avora said. "Don't explain what you're going to do. Do it! These are the tryouts, dear. This is it."

I licked my lips.

I began the poem over again. The third time! Was that a mistake?

" 'To Arnold With Whom I Used To Pick Raspberries When We Were Children Thirty-five Years Ago.

" 'Arnold, you were a fool to shoot yourself: Social arrangements aren't everything.' "

I paused, suddenly remembering that I was supposed to use my hands expressively.

" 'Even if your wife threw you out,' "

(I made a throwing motion.)

" 'Even if your own children turned their backs on you,' "

(I turned my head sharply.)

" 'You should have lived to spite them.

The trouble is you never learned

More than the human species matters.' "

I stumbled here, because all at once I remembered that I was also supposed to use my *voice* expressively. I almost groaned out loud, but swallowed it up with a cough.

I put as much feeling as I could into the last two lines. That was where I always wanted to cry.

" '*Now* I'll pick for *myself* the raspberries that you can't pick.

The reddest ones are just as good as last year's.' "

I stopped.

"That's it?" Mrs. Avora asked.

"Yes. The end." I wiped my eyes.

Laredo clapped really hard.

Mrs. Avora said, "Lovely poem. Thank you, Danita," and wrote something in her notebook. "Next," she called. "Denise Bright."

" 'Hark!' " Denise Bright was saying as Laredo and I walked out of the auditorium, " 'Is that the morning sun yonder?' "

"So what do you think?" I asked Laredo. "How'd I do?" She squeezed my arm in a consoling way. "It was that bad?" I said.

"Maybe you can do backstage stuff for Greasepaint, work on sets or costumes . . ."

"Maybe," I sighed.

"It's an alternate plan," Laredo said. "It's always a good idea to have an alternate plan.

That's what I do when things go wrong, Dani. I have an alternate plan."

"I guess you're right." Why had I set my heart on Greasepaint?

"I *am* right," Laredo said. "I told you my father wrote that he's sending me airline tickets for Thanksgiving?"

"You'll finally get to meet your baby brother."

"*Maybe,*" Laredo said. "Remember last spring? Remember where I was supposed to go — Texas? Remember where I was — right here? See what I mean about alternate plans? If my father doesn't come through with the tickets *again*, instead of being depressed, I'm going to go out and do something really nice for myself."

"Like what?"

"I don't know yet, but I'll figure it out. I was talking to Geo about it last night."

Geo was Laredo's other friend. They had "met" over the summer when he dialed the wrong number. If it had been me he dialed, I would have hung up. But not Laredo. "I liked the sound of his voice," she'd told me. She talked to him for an hour that first time. Now, almost every week, either she phoned him or he phoned her. But they still hadn't met face to face.

"He was so cute last night," she said, "all excited about whales. He's reading about them for a project for his biology class. Did you know that the tongue of a blue whale weighs as much as an elephant?"

I shook my head.

"Did you know that so-called killer whales are

actually totally friendly and like to have their bellies scratched?"

"I might have heard about that."

"Did you know that humpback whales sing?"

"Yes. I've heard their songs on a record. My father borrowed it from a friend of his to play for us once."

Laredo linked her arm with mine. "You knew that? You're so smart. I didn't know any of it."

Chapter 5

"We had Greasepaint tryouts yesterday," I said at supper the next night. "I blew it. I'm not going to make it in."

"It was good you tried out," Lizbeth said. She dug into her Jell-O. "It's good to try out things."

"Yeah, thanks." She was quoting Mom.

"Sweetie!" Mom said. "You really blew it?" She gave me a warm, tender look. I wished she wouldn't do that! I knew she was being sympathetic, but it made me feel as if she thought I'd fall apart if she were just matter-of-fact.

Dad wasn't much better. "Don't worry, Dani, acting isn't your thing, anyway," he said.

But that was the point! I'd finally figured out why I'd wanted to make Greasepaint — to prove to myself that I *could* do something that wasn't "my thing."

"But since you tried out," he went on, giving me his version of Mom's warm, tender look, "you can't let it crush you if you didn't make it, sweetheart."

Thank goodness the phone rang just then. One more drop of sympathy and I'd probably melt into a puddle! I pushed back my chair. "I'll get it; it's probably Laredo." I rushed into the kitchen and shut the door. "Hi, Laredo," I said, picking up, "what are you doing? Am I glad you called! My family — "

"Uh, excuse me," a male voice broke in, "I'm calling for the head of the house."

"Oh! Excuse *me!*" My cheeks got red. "Is this you, Mr. Homan?" He was the foreman in Dad's print shop. It sounded sort of like him.

"Uh, no, this is not — " He coughed. "Is the head of the household in?"

"I'll get him," I said. "Who should I say is calling?"

"A friend. Say a friend, for Mr. Marrin."

"For who?"

"Mr. Daniel Marrin. Is this his home?"

"Do you want Daniel *Merritt?*"

"Merritt? Umm, I might. Have I made a mistake? I have this name someone gave me. He's an old friend of my, uh, stepfather's and he asked me to look him up."

"Daniel *Merritt?*" I repeated.

"Who is this?" he said.

"This is Danita Merritt, the daughter."

"Oh, I see. Let me check this name. Daniel . . . Marrin."

24

"Sorry, you have the wrong number."

"You're sure?" He had a nice voice, deep and kind of calm. Now that I heard it, I was really embarrassed that I'd thought it might be Mr. Homan's. Mr. Homan was old! This voice was much younger. "D. Marrin?" he repeated. "You sure he doesn't live here?"

I laughed. "I ought to be sure. *I* live here."

He was laughing, too. "I didn't mean to doubt your word! It's just, I want to be one hundred percent sure. I told my stepfather I'd look up this old friend. So this isn't six five six, two two one three?"

"This is six five six, two two one *one*."

"I guess I made another mistake. Sorry about that."

"That's okay," I said again, "you were close, anyway."

"But no brass rings, right? Well, thanks a lot."

"You're welcome. 'Bye."

" 'Bye," he said. But he didn't hang up. "Oh, uh, would you know where a good place to rent a car is? I'm new in town, and — "

"Out at the airport, I think. When my father has a trip to make, he always rents a car at the airport."

Maybe he was trying to keep the conversation going. Maybe it was like Geo and Laredo. Except I wouldn't get away with it; my parents would never let me be friends, not even phone friends, with someone they didn't know.

"Is there a bus going out there?" he asked. "Would you know that?"

25

"I'm not sure. I could ask my father for you. You want to wait, and I'll just go ask — "

"No, no, no, that's okay. I shouldn't keep you any longer. Thanks a lot for your help. I really appreciate it."

"Sure, you're welcome. 'Bye," I said again. "Good luck in finding Mr. Marrin," I remembered to say, but he'd already hung up.

Later, I looked up Daniel Marrin in the phone book. No Daniel Marrin. No D. Marrin. No one with a name even close to Dad's with a phone number off by only one digit. Maybe I'd heard wrong. Had he asked for Daniel *Harrin*? Or Daniel *Sarren*?

After puzzling over it a little while, I let it go. I forgot the phone call and the funny coincidence of names. Why would I remember it? It had been a mistake. Of course it had been a little different than the usual wrong-number call, in that we'd practically had a whole conversation. And he'd had such a nice voice! But that was still no reason for me to remember it.

Chapter 6

Friday after school, the list of people who'd made it into Greasepaint went up on the bulletin board on the first floor near the office. I stood with Laredo, looking for my name. LAWSON, RUDY. MONAGO, HILARY. OPECITO, PAUL . . . If I'd gotten in, my name would have been right there between LAWSON, RUDY and MONAGO, HILARY. MERRITT, DANITA. I must have read that list ten times.

"Let's go," Laredo said. We went out and crossed over to Division. We were going to Laredo's house. It was warm, the air smelled of leaves and smoke.

"I'd like to know what I did wrong . . ." I kept chewing over the tryouts. "I didn't realize for a while you were giving me the signal to talk louder. . . . I bet I blew it right then. . . . I suppose I should be relieved I didn't make it. If I had to get out on a stage in front of a real audience, I probably wouldn't survive."

Laredo made a clicking sound in her teeth. "Dani, *you* didn't expect to make it. *I* didn't expect you to make it. Plus, you've had two days to get used to the idea that you wouldn't make it, so give it a rest."

Why didn't I pick up on her voice, the rush of irritated words? Then I wouldn't have been caught by surprise later. Well, I wasn't being my most observant self. Actually, I was being completely self-centered.

Laredo unlocked the downstairs door next to the People's Beer Hall, and we went up. Inside, we took off our shoes (one of Mrs. Gerardi's rules) and went into the kitchen. I helped myself to a soda. "I just hope Mom and Dad don't make a big fuss and try to make me feel better."

Laredo made another clicking sound. It flickered through my mind that it wasn't a sympathetic click. I half knew I was going on and on about Greasepaint. I still went on and on.

"I know my parents mean well. They'll probably figure out some special treat just to help me feel better. . . . They should leave me alone, let me work things out myself. I shouldn't have told them today was the day I'd find out for sure."

"You have such terrible problems." Laredo was sitting on the counter and banging her heels.

"I guess I should start thinking about working backstage. At least you don't have to try out for that," I said.

"Are you always going to slink around life, Dani?" *Bang bang*.

I put down my soda. "Hello? Excuse me?"

Laredo pushed her hair behind her ears. "It's disgusting the way you operate," she tossed off. "If backstage was your first choice, okay . . . but since it isn't, it's just *settling*."

Music drifted up through the floor from the bar below, sounding a little tinny the way music does when you hear it from a distance. "Settling?" I repeated.

"Yes. Settling, as in 'second best.' "

"Laredo, you were the one who gave me the idea of working backstage. The alternate plan . . . remember?"

"Oh, please." *Bang bang*. "Taking Greasepaint so seriously . . . what a big fuss over completely nothing!"

"You're mad at me," I said.

"I am not!"

"Why are you mad at me?"

"I don't want to talk about it."

"Laredo, talk to me."

"No! Just go home."

"Laredo — "

"No!"

"Laredo — "

"Shut up! Get out! Let's call the whole thing off!"

"What whole thing?"

"Us." She banged her heels.

"*Us?* Are you crazy? You mean our friendship?"

29

"Yes!" *BANG BANG BANG.* "Yes. Yes!" She leaned forward on her hands. Her face was flushed. "When you think about it, we don't have anything in common. I mean, you and your cozy family with all their gooey sympathy. It just makes me sick!"

"Laredo — you don't mean it."

"I do!"

I got my jacket and books. "You're going to make a stinking doctor. Good doctors have feelings, they're not cold and heartless."

"The door's over there."

I picked up my shoes and walked out barefoot.

I'd seen Laredo like this once before, a few months after we met. Her father was supposed to be flying east to see her. She'd been almost beside herself with excitement. Every time she'd talked about his visit, her face flushed, her hair stood out all over. Then the day she was expecting him, she got a telegram. She showed it to me. " 'Had to turn back in Chicago. Beverly sick. Very sorry. Love, Dad.' "

" 'Love, Dad,' " she mimicked. "His precious wifey is sick!" And then, *"Shut up,"* she'd said to me, although I was only thinking of things to say and hadn't said anything yet.

She apologized later. "Something happened to me. I just felt so crazy — it just came over me," she'd said. And I'd said, "That's okay, that's all right." I felt sorry for her. She really missed her father.

Now I wondered, was it her father again? Something told me it was. But something also told me, *So what!* So what if it was her father? So what if it was her mother this time? Or twelve tiny women with purple horns and pink tails? Did being upset give her the right to act that way, to declare our friendship *kaput* and order me out of her life?

At home, I wandered around feeling empty. My disappointment about Greasepaint seemed minor compared to the fight with Laredo. Was that what it had been, a fight? It seemed more like an earthquake. Except an earthquake was an act of nature. This was an act of Laredo's.

Once or twice I looked out the window. What did I expect to see — Laredo, walking down the street, coming to apologize? There was nobody out there except a boy leaning against a tree across the street. I wouldn't have even noticed him if he hadn't been bundled up in a jacket, a hat, and a scarf half wound around his face. Why was he wearing all those clothes on such a warm day?

A little later, I looked again, and he was still there. Why was he looking at our house? What was he doing, snooping on us? Suddenly, I ran out the door, down the walk, and straight across the street. He seemed to almost jump in the air when he saw me coming. I got a glimpse of red sneakers. And then he was gone.

Chapter 7

Saturday, Mom drove me to the dentist. She was going on from there with Lizbeth to the stables. "You sure you don't want me to pick you up later, Danita?" The third time she'd asked me the same thing.

"I don't want to wait around for you."

"Kirstie and I are riding for one full hour on the trails," Lizbeth said. She was wearing her riding breeches and high, black rubber boots. She swished her riding crop. "And then I'm going to brush and curry King Abo Spring Morning. And I'm mucking, too. Mrs. Sandler-Frost said I could help muck out the stalls today."

"No matter how long I live, I will never understand why my sister considers it a privilege to shovel horse manure," I said.

"Well, that's your problem, Dani."

"Oh, thank you, Lizbeth, I'm sure it's normal to want to play in horse manure."

"I don't *play* in it — "

"Are you going to go to the mall afterward, sweetie?" Mom interrupted.

"Maybe."

I should have just said no. Now Mom would ask if I had enough money with me, what I was going to buy, and then tell me if I got hungry to be sure to get myself something to eat, but not junk, something nourishing. And she'd say, *You're growing, it's not good for you to go too long a time without nourishment.*

". . . growing, and it's not a good idea for you to go hours and hours without some food. Food is fuel, Danita."

Oops, I almost forgot that part. I had my hand on the door handle. "Is that it, Mom?"

"I love you."

"I love you, too." I did, but did I have to say it every time she did?

"Good luck, sweetheart. Hope you don't have any cavities."

Well, I did. Two of them. "Just little ones," Dr. V. said, with his big cheery smile. It wasn't his teeth that had to be drilled.

I'd had some idea of hanging around the mall afterward, getting a glimpse or two of Jon, but when I left Dr. V.'s, my jaw was frozen and I was slobbering out of the corner of my mouth. I took the bus straight home.

I was lying on my bed, reading, when the phone rang. I went across the hall to Mom and

Dad's room and sat down on their bed. "Hello?"

"Is Mr. Merritt in?"

"No." I rubbed my jaw.

"Is this his daughter?"

"Yes."

There was a cough across the line. "I thought so. How old are you again?"

"Excuse me?" I wiped my mouth with the back of my hand. "Who did you say this was?"

"This is a friend of your father's. Is your brother there?"

"Who?"

"You have a brother, don't you?"

"No." I felt like saying, *Maybe you're mixing me up with my girlfriend! Laredo has a brother*. Just thinking that, just thinking of Laredo's name, I got a burning feeling in my chest.

"Oh, I'm sorry," the caller said. "I was sure you had a — "

I looked at the phone. His voice sounded so familiar. "Did you call before?" I asked.

"What? . . . Just tell your father I called. Thanks." He hung up.

"Hey!" I said to the silent phone. "How can I tell him you called if you didn't leave your name?"

That night Dad and Mom decided to take me and Lizbeth to the movies. "I'd rather stay home," I said.

"But you love the movies." Automatically, my mother put the back of her hand against my forehead to test for fever.

Dad pushed my bangs off my face. They were

at it again, hovering over me like two anxious helicopters. "What will you do all alone?" Dad said, as if I couldn't spend two minutes of my life without company.

"I'll read. I'll watch TV. I'll be fine. I'd just like to be by myself tonight." I was proud of how calm I sounded. But not calm enough for my mother.

She gazed at me. "You look sort of flushed. How does your jaw feel? Now that I think of it, you were kind of mopey this morning."

"I was not! I felt great all day." A bald-faced lie, but what was I supposed to say? *You're right! I was mopey! I felt rotten! How would you feel if your best friend went crazy and turned your friendship into a heap of rubble?*

"You can tell me your feelings, Danita," Lizbeth said. Great! Helicopter number three had just buzzed into action. "Talking about feelings helps you feel better," the Little Therapist went on.

"Where did you learn that?" I asked.

"A lady came to our school to talk about emotions."

"Okay, you talk about *your* emotions."

"I try to. Right now I feel very cheerful because Mommy and Daddy are taking us to a movie."

My father laughed. "How'd I ever get along without you girls?" He gave Lizbeth a hug, then me. "You really don't want to come to this movie, Dani?"

"No, Dad. Please."

So they went without me. A tiny victory. I

35

could brood in peace. I thought about seeing Laredo in school Monday. Usually we rushed up to each other. *Ta, Laredo! Ta, Dani!* And maybe that's just how it would be. We'd hug, and Laredo would say, *That was all nothing, it was idiotic!* Then another hug, and the fight would be over. No questions asked.

Chapter 8

Monday, in school, Laredo and I walked, not rushed, toward each other. One cool glance and that was it. In gym, we were on the same volleyball team, but we didn't talk then, either. Not a word. Not a single syllable. Which is not to say I wasn't thinking a million things.

Laredo, pretend it's twenty years from now and we're grown up, and we've got careers, and we're married, and we have children, and we've never made up our fight! Then one day we see each other. And you know what? You feel rotten. You know what a big mistake you made twenty years ago! You cry buckets, you want to make up NOW, but guess what, it's too late! It doesn't do you any good!

It's really strange breaking up with your best friend. The worst part is the way you feel. The second-worst part is that you have so much time on your hands. That's probably why I got up my courage finally and went to a meeting of Greasepaint to ask if I could work with the backstage crew.

Mrs. Avora touched her cap of black hair. "Well . . . we can always use another pair of hands. Shirley Larkin, what do you think?"

A tall, beautiful girl with very red lips came over and asked my name and homeroom. "Well, fine," she said.

I waited. I thought I'd be put to work on something right away, something important like painting scenery or working on costumes. "Is that it?" I said.

"For now." I could tell from the way Shirley Larkin smiled that she was at least a junior, maybe even a senior. "What did you expect?" she said kindly, as if speaking to someone very young and not too bright.

I gave her a big smile and left, wishing Laredo was there to tell me I'd acted okay and hadn't made a fool of myself.

Thursday after school, I went to the mall with a shopping list Mom had given me. I walked into Strawberries, and right away I saw Laredo in front of the makeup counter. She saw me, too, but she dropped her eyes, as if she hadn't seen me, or as if I didn't exist. Take your pick. Then she left.

I stood there, balancing for a moment between feeling sorry for myself and getting mad. Mad won, and I went charging out of the store after Laredo. I was going to get her and tell her a thing or two. *Laredo, you're trying to cancel out our friendship, but I've got news for you. You can't make it disappear. We made something that wasn't in the world before. Understand? It's the friendship of Laredo and Danita, and it's a real thing. Maybe you can't see it, but it's real anyway. And it's always going to be out there, somewhere. Think about that, Laredo!*

Somebody bumped into me; stepped on my heel, actually. "Sorry," a boy behind me said. "That was clumsy of me."

Just what I'd thought, but since he'd said it, I couldn't.

"You okay?" He was wearing white pants and a loose cotton shirt. His hair was cut short on top, but with a thin ponytail at his neck. "I'm sorry." He kept apologizing and looking at me. "I'm really sorry — "

"It's okay, it's *okay*," I said. I glanced into the crowd ahead of me. I'd lost Laredo. Shoot! I moved aside so the boy could pass me. For some reason, I looked down. Bare ankles. Red sneakers. No socks. Could this be the same boy Laredo and I had noticed staring at us last week? Suddenly, I thought of the guy who'd been standing across from our house Saturday morning. The one with the scarf wrapped around his face. And red sneakers. Were they the same red sneakers?

Ask him! Ask him if he's the same one as the one with the scarf. I could hear Laredo's voice. *Action, not contemplation, Dani.*

Oh, shut up, Laredo! I thought. I turned aside and went down the stairs and found myself in front of Ice Dreams. Jon was there, behind the

39

counter. I went in, just did it without thinking. Action, not contemplation.

"Can I help you?" Jon said.

"Uh." I stood against the counter, looking up at the menu of different flavors. "P-pistachio, please."

"Cone or dish?"

"Uh, c-cone." I'd never stuttered in my life, but now I couldn't seem to stop.

"Large or small?"

"Uh, s-small."

He dipped the ice cream, smoothed the cool green mound with the back of the silver dipper, then handed me the cone with a napkin wrapped around it. "One dollar, please."

I gave him the money, took a lick of the ice cream.

"See you around," he said. And he gave me his beautiful smile.

I walked out, dazed, thinking I'd done just what Laredo had been urging me to do . . . and she wasn't even around to applaud.

Chapter 9

Just as I walked into homeroom, the PA buzzed, and a voice said, "Good morning, all. This is Bunny Larrabee with today's exciting announcements! It is Friday, October tenth."

October tenth? I slid into my seat. It was Laredo's birthday! We should have been celebrating instead of passing in the hall with our *I see you but I wish I didn't* stare.

I told myself, *Don't think about it!* But I couldn't help myself. I thought about how much fun we'd had last year on her birthday, how everything had been so perfect. I'd bought her a bunny-fur sweater, which she said she'd wanted forever. We'd had all her favorite food. Lamb chops, sweet potatoes, chocolate-mocha cake. We'd watched a movie, stuffed ourselves on ice cream and more cake, and argued — or laughed, I should say — over who was going to sleep on the floor.

I said, "Laredo, it's your birthday, *I* take the floor."

She said, "Dani, I get the bed every night."

"No way! You're the birthday girl."

"You're the guest! The bed is yours!"

Eventually we agreed to share the bed. As Laredo said later, "*Extremo* mistake." Her bed is old, the springs creak every time you move a toe, and no matter how you try to clutch the sides, the mattress (and you with it) sinks in the middle like quicksand. Instead of falling asleep, we kept falling into each other.

Around four o'clock in the morning, too exhausted to laugh anymore and hours after her mother had told us to quiet down, we finally fell asleep. We didn't wake up until nearly noon. Too late for school, of course. Boo hoo! We made waffles, bacon, toast, and coffee. Coffee! My parents never allowed me that. Or skipping school, especially if it was my own fault that I'd overslept. Laredo and I had agreed it was the greatest thirteenth birthday anyone could have.

Bunny Larrabee was making another announcement. "This is to remind you all of the Mixer in the gym at noon. Everyone come and bring your school spirit with you! And now, before we close, a little joke to start your day off right. . . . What did the overweight man say to the skinny woman?" She paused. "I'll go on a diet when I stop believing in the survival of the fattest."

42

The whole class groaned.

Laredo and I had planned to go to the Mixer. Now I decided to skip it. Mixers were for being silly, laughing, dancing, meeting people, and having fun. What was the opposite of all that? Gloom, woe, and grief? Must be, because that was how I felt. But passing the gym on my way to the lunchroom, I peeked in . . . and I saw Jon inside. And my feet took charge, turned, and walked me right in. It was like Ice Dreams the other day. Gliding in there in a kind of dream.

Jon was standing near one of the basketball hoops. My feet kept moving me in that direction.

"Hi, Danita," someone said.

"Hi." Smile.

Mrs. Jones-Barbarra, our vice-principal, was speaking into a mike. "May I have a volunteer to man — sorry — I mean, *people* the record player? And, girls, don't forget, you can ask the boys to dance."

Now I was near enough Jon to stop and stare. *See you around.* Hadn't those been his exact words? What if he meant he'd see me *here?* I wished . . . I didn't know *what* I wished. Something about Jon and me. Could I ask him to dance? He was a boy. I was a girl. Hadn't Mrs. Jones-Barbarra just said . . . My heart raced. I couldn't! I didn't have the nerve.

I walked around the gym, around and around, thinking about Jon. I didn't want to fling myself all over him. Not exactly. But . . . what if we were alone . . . and he wanted to kiss me? Just the thought of it made me go weak. Why does one person do that to you and not another? If I could ask Laredo, I knew what she'd say. *Dani, if you like him, do something about it.*

I walked around the gym one more time. That was when I saw Jon dancing with Shirley Larkin. Shirley Larkin and Jon! I stopped and stared at them, at their two blond heads, their golden skin, their white, white smiles. "Shirley Larkin . . . Jon Haberle." I whispered their names to myself.

He was beautiful. He was glamorous. He was special.

So was she!

How could I ever hope *anything* about Jon and me? I couldn't.

Then, at the exact moment I thought that, Jon glanced over Shirley's shoulder, looked at me . . . and winked!

I didn't know what it meant. Did he remember me? Did he like me? Did he think I was cute? Did he like me as much as he liked Shirley? Or maybe . . . even . . . *more?*

I felt dazed and weird for the rest of the day, half of me gloomy over Laredo, the other half of me dazzled by Jon Haberle and his wink.

I saw Shirley in the hall, and I was going to walk past her, but she called me. "Hi," I said. I looked up, then down. My face got hot. Did she know Jon had winked at me?

"How about coming to work with the crew after school today?" she said.

I stared at her red fingernails. It took a moment

for the words to sink in. What had I been expecting her to say? *I know about you and Jon, and I'm telling you right now — back off!*

I held my books against my chest. "What should I bring?"

"Yourself and your legs. We'll run you into the ground."

"Shirley, don't scare her," Trudy Marsh said, stopping. She was another junior girl in Greasepaint. She had big brown freckles all over her face and arms. She gave me a nice smile. But later, backstage, she was the one who really sent me scurrying!

For two hours that afternoon I was your basic gofer, running around with glasses of water and picking up screwdrivers and sweaters and paintbrushes. In between, I swept up around the people working on the sets.

Trudy Marsh put two fingers in her mouth and whistled. "Dani. Yo, Dani!" She was standing on top of a ladder, painting a stormy sky on a section of set. "Wake up, girl. That's the third time I called you."

"Sorry . . ." My cheeks were hot. I'd gone off into a daydream about Jon.

"Are you present now? Hand me up that paintbrush." She pointed. I didn't see the paintbrush. "Help," she moaned.

Shirley took my head between her hands and turned it in the right direction. "Lucky us," she murmured.

Meaning *unlucky* them, to get stuck with me? My cheeks got hotter. I took several deep breaths. Then a new thought hit me. What if Shirley said something to Jon about me?

Jon, we have this new girl working backstage. What an airhead. You have to call her three times to get her attention. She can't see a paintbrush that's under her nose. She gets red in the face every time you talk to her. Total loss.

And what if Jon nodded understandingly.

I think I know who you mean, Shirley. Is she skinny? Does she stammer? Does she like, ugh, pistachio ice cream?

I swept furiously in a corner.

I remembered the way Shirley and Jon had danced at the Mixer, their arms around each other. Were they going together? Of course they were! They were a perfect couple. He'd probably given her his class ring. They'd probably pledged eternal love.

I swept harder.

Then I remembered Jon winking at me over Shirley's shoulder.

And I didn't know what to think.

Chapter 10

I wandered around school during lunch period, hoping to see Jon. I looked in the music room. (He played drums in the band.) I looked in the office. I looked in the gym. And there, I saw not Jon, but Laredo. She was sitting in the bleachers, and there were two boys at her feet in attitudes of adoration. I knew them. I'd known them all my life. Davis and Ronnie Buck, cousins, two of the worst pests in the universe.

Laredo laughed at something one of them said, pushing her hair behind her ears. Great. My ex-best friend preferred the company of two of the biggest creeps in creation to mine! What bad taste!

I felt like saying that to her.

I walked into the gym and looked up at Laredo. But then I didn't say anything, just stood there and stared at her.

Maybe she knew what was in my mind. She lifted her chin and looked the other way.

Ronnie Buck was the one who looked at me. He had a big spotted face like a toad. "Merritt! What are you doing here?"

"Your mouth's hanging open," his cousin, Davis, giggled.

Ronnie flicked his hand at me. "Vamoose, girl. Amscray. Can't you see the b-i-i-i-g people are busy?"

I opened my mouth to say something, but before I could, Laredo put her foot against Ronnie's back. "What did you say?"

"I'm telling the Merritt to vamoose."

"*The Merritt?*" Laredo said.

Davis and Ronnie both giggled.

"I have a better idea. Why don't you two vamoose?"

"Awwww, Laredo," they whined.

"Good-bye, Ronnie. Good-bye, Davis." She waved her hand, dismissing them. She was like a queen waving them away. And away they went!

I thought I should say something, like, *Thanks for cleaning up the atmosphere.* Or maybe, *Great performance!* "Laredo!" I said.

"What!"

"Isn't this stupid?"

"Isn't *what* stupid?"

"This whole thing with us! I think it's really ridiculous and *stupid.*"

After a moment, she said, "I'll buy that."

"At least we agree on something."

"Yeah," she said, "something."

Was this progress? I said, "Do you want to talk about it?"

She rolled her shoulders around. "Maybe."

"Yes or no, Laredo?"

She sighed deeply. *Y-e-e-s!* But not here."

"Where, then? Outside?"

"Fine!"

Just like that, we were walking out of the gym, out of school, and around the back of the building. The girls' track team was out doing sprints. We started climbing the hill behind the school. Neither of us said anything.

"I went to the Mixer," I said, to start things off.

"I didn't."

"I saw Jon there. And Shirley Larkin. Do you know her? They were dancing together." I forgot to be cool, and blurted, "She's beautiful! You should see them together."

"Oh, phoo! She's probably not a quarter as smart as you."

"Laredo, how sexist." But I couldn't help smiling. "She's smart, she's got talent, she's got everything."

"So do you," Laredo said, sounding just like she always used to, loyal and warm and loving.

I'd had all this strong stuff to say to her, and suddenly I didn't care. I only wanted things to be the way they used to be. "Why can't our fight just be over with?" I said.

"That's all right with me," Laredo said.

"It is?"

"Yes!"

We smiled at each other.

"You saw me that day in Strawberries, didn't you?" I said.

"Yeah, I did."

"I knew it. I followed you — "

"I didn't see you."

"Well, this guy bumped into me — no, wait a second, I don't want to tell you that yet. If we're made up, we should hug and make it official first." So we did. And I suddenly felt really happy.

We got to the top of the hill and sat down under the trees. You could see the school and half the city spread out below. "Well, will you tell me why it happened?" I asked.

"Do I have to talk about it?"

"You don't have to, Laredo, but I wish you would. You really hurt me when you told me we should forget being friends. What was that, a whim or something?"

"Dan-i! No. It was . . . I don't know! I don't understand myself. It happened because I was in a foul, ugly mood, and . . . I let it happen." She slumped over. "Let me tell you one thing, though, it wasn't a *whim*."

"What was it?"

"Despair," she said, with a crooked smile. "I could tell you the whole deal, but it's all bla bla bla bla and the same old stuff. My father."

"I thought so! What'd he do now?"

"No Thanksgiving trip." She gave me that crooked smile again. "He called me that morning, said Thanksgiving wasn't going to be a convenient time for him after all. . . . I guess I went a little bananas. I knew I was taking my feelings out on you, but somehow I just . . . didn't care."

"This isn't the first time it happened, Laredo."

"I'm sorry," she said quietly. "I wouldn't blame you if you gave up on me. Do you hate me?"

"No. And I'm never going to give up on you. You don't give up on people you love. Only, tell me one thing. If I hadn't come over to you in the gym today, would it have been Strawberries all over again? You running away from me, saying nothing?"

She shook her head. "I was going to talk to you. I was! . . . It was a miserable week without you, Dani." She took my thumb and matched it up against hers. "I knew we couldn't be broken up forever. You knew it, too, didn't you?"

I nodded. "I knew it."

Chapter 11

"This is going to be the first time my little brother has ever actually seen me," Laredo said. We entered the mall by one of the side entrances. It was Saturday morning. "I'm just a name to him. I mean, I *hope* I'm a name to him. I don't even know if I'm that much. I don't know what my father has told him about me. Does Jasper even know he has a sister?"

"He will, once he gets the video," I said.

Laredo hugged my arm. "This is such a brilliant idea! I don't know how you came up with it."

We got on the escalator to ground level. "Laredo, all I did was say you should send your little brother a video of you."

"I know! That's what I said. It was brilliant, Dani."

I smiled modestly. Right near You Can Be a Star, Too, there was a full-length mirror. Laredo slowed down to look herself over, and I peered over her shoulder. I'd fixed my hair in a new style that morning, pulling it all to one side, very slick and smooth. I thought it made me look older.

The front of You Can Be a Star, Too was just a tiny room with a counter, a video monitor, and three straight chairs. There was a door in the far wall. A woman in a silver dress came through the door, and Laredo told her what she wanted to do.

"You want to talk? Just talk? You don't want to sing?" the woman said. "Everybody wants to sing or play an instrument."

"I want to send a message."

The woman shrugged. "Your choice." She pushed open the door. "Let's go back here into the studio."

I started to go with them, but Laredo said, "No, Dani, you can wait for me." I sat down. I didn't mind. I knew exactly what Laredo was going to say. I had heard her practice at least half a dozen times this morning.

Hi, Jasper! This is your sister, Laredo. I think it's neat that I have a little brother. I want to get to know you. I'm planning to call you up soon and talk to you. I hope you'll tell me all about yourself. What kind of games do you like to play? Some things I like to do are play science games and go to movies and spend time with my best friend. Her name is Danita . . .

A boy came out from the back and went behind the counter. "Well, hi," he said.

I stared. It was Red Sneakers, the boy with the ponytail and the bare ankles. "Didn't you bump into me the other day?" I blurted.

He leaned over the counter. "Yeah . . . it was you, wasn't it? I guess I did. Sorry about that; I'm not usually so clumsy." He had a nice smile. "What are you doing here?"

"Waiting for my friend. What about you?"

"I work here. Are you going to make a video, too, Dani?"

"How'd you know my name?"

"I, uh, heard your friend talking to you."

"Oh." Had he been listening to us?

"I'm D.T. Goodman," he said.

"I'm Dani Merritt."

"I *know!*"

"You didn't know my last name."

"Well . . ." He gave me a cute grin. "I'm from California. Maybe that makes me intuitive. . . . I've only been out here three weeks, but I've done okay. I've got a room at the Y and I've got this job."

"Where do you come from in California?"

"Bakersfield. Did you ever hear of it? Marilyn Monroe lived there once. Claim to fame! It's totally different there. Dry. Hot. I like it here okay. The trees are fabulous, man! Winter's coming. I'm looking forward to that. I ski. Some people don't know we ski in California. You have to go up into the mountains. California has everything!"

I had the stupid idea that he was telling me

54

this stuff because I had changed my hairstyle. I wanted to ask him how old he thought I was, but I lost my nerve and just said, "Don't you go to school?"

"I should be in my second year of college. I took a leave to come here. That was my main desire — to come east — but I probably will eventually go back to college."

"What for? I mean, what will you study?"

"Marine biology. I'm attracted to that."

I tried to think of something intelligent to say. I had to settle for, "How old are you?"

"Nineteen. How old are you, Dani?"

"Almost fourteen."

He peered at me. "That's what I thought."

"Oh." I was disappointed. Maybe I'd have to change my hairdo again.

"My mom comes from around here," he said. "Menands, little burg south of this town."

"Menands? My father grew up there, too. My grandparents lived there until they moved to Florida."

"I got my start in life there," he said.

"You were born there, too?"

"No, not that. . . . You know what I mean."

Did I? Sort of. I didn't want to act dumb, though, so I nodded as if I understood perfectly.

"So what kind of guy is your father?" he said. "I mean, coming from a small town, and all . . ."

The way he jumped around from one thing to another! "My girlfriend says he's a ten as a dad. How about yours?"

"My stepfather? An okay guy, but the relationship is not too profound. So you like your father?"

"Yes, of course. But — "

"But what?"

"Oh, nothing."

He leaned across the counter. My face got warm. He was looking at me so intently.

"Well . . . he hovers too much. Worries about me, if I'm going to get sick, stuff like that. I was a preemie, but that was years ago."

"My mother worries about me, too," he said. "She thinks I'm impulsive. I tried to tell her dropping out of college wasn't an impulse. I thought about it before I did it. But one thing that's excellent about my mother, she believes in independence. She trusts me."

I didn't know what to say to that. It was like a reproach to me. Did my parents trust me? I was glad that Laredo and the woman in the silver dress came through the door just then.

"She was very good," the woman said, going behind the counter and making out a bill.

Laredo took out her wallet. "I did it in just two takes, Dani." She smiled at D.T., then looked at me with her eyebrows raised, like *Wooo! Cute!*

"Don't you remember him?" I said when we left. "I'm sure he's the one who gave you the big stare that day we came over here to see Jon."

"Really?"

"But the funny thing is, I keep bumping into him. I think I even saw him on my street."

"Maybe he lives there."

"No, he's living in the Y."

"How do you know that?"

We crossed the parking lot to the post office on Kinney Road so Laredo could mail the cassette out to her brother right away. "He told me," I said.

"Well, he's quite adorable. Who cares where he lives?"

Chapter 12

"Dani, I got a job," Laredo said the moment she sat down in the lunchroom. "I told them I was sixteen. And wait till you hear where I'm working. You won't guess in a million years. Ice Dreams."

I almost choked on my apple. "The same place Jon works?"

"Yes. I am in such a good mood, Dani! I'm going to make so much money. More than I ever did baby-sitting. I'll never have to buy my clothes on sale again."

"But, Laredo, didn't they want to see your working papers?"

"I told the manager I'd bring them in next week. I figure he'll forget by then. What does he care how old I am, as long as I do my job? I'll be a good worker."

I won't lie, I felt envious of Laredo's independence and guts. I would never have the nerve and confidence to talk my way into a job like that.

"You know something else that's great about this job, Dani? I can put in a word for you with Jon. It's a perfect opportunity. I could be just casual about it and — "

"No, no, no! I don't want you to do that, Laredo. Don't say anything about me to Jon."

"Why? If I did, it would only be good."

"No, don't even mention my name! I think he and Shirley are going together. She's wearing a ring on a chain around her neck! I'm sure it means they're steady now."

"Ohhhh." Laredo said it as if she felt every bit as bad as I did. "I'm sorry, Dani."

After school, we walked over to the mall. I should say, we hustled over. Laredo barely had enough time to get to work. I sat down at one of the little tables with the red-and-blue Cinzano umbrellas and opened my notebook. I could see Laredo — and Jon — perfectly from where I was. Maybe he'd look around . . . his eyes would meet my eyes. . . . And suddenly, he'd know Shirley was a terrible mistake. He'd walk toward me . . . and he'd be saying my name . . . *Dani . . . Dani . . .*

I made myself open my history book and concentrate on American gunboats in China a century ago. People passed. I didn't look up. Someone pulled out the chair across from me. I kept reading. Then a hand fell across my book. "Hi there, Dani."

It was D.T. Goodman. He put down a sandwich wrapped in paper. "My supper," he said. "Mind if I eat it here?" He turned a chair around and sat down with his arms across the back. "Do you live in this mall, or what?"

I blushed. "My girlfriend has a job here. I'm just keeping her company. In a manner of speaking."

"I get it. That's nice," he said. "Where does she work?" I pointed to Ice Dreams, and he looked over. "She's the cute one with the blonde hair?"

"No, that's Jon! A boy."

D.T. grinned. Oh! He was teasing me. I blushed harder.

He took a swallow from a carton of milk and then a bite of his sandwich. "I'd offer you some of this, but I figure you have supper waiting at home."

Was that a question?

"Dani, do you know what are the two most important things in life?"

I thought, *Sure I do! Love and . . .* But then I couldn't think what the second thing was.

"You want to know the answer? Luck and jokes."

"Not love?"

"Well . . . that's important. But it's not enough. Your whole life is actually about luck.

Good luck. Bad luck. I've had some good luck, some bad luck. Jokes are important to help you keep your balance when you find out about the bad luck."

"I never thought of it that way."

"Now you'll never forget."

He was easy to be with, but where had he come from — and I didn't mean Bakersfield, California. He seemed to have just walked into my life and started talking to me like I was an old friend. Was this the way people were in California — casual, friendly, relaxed?

"Dani, do you have brothers and sisters?"

"One sister, Lizbeth. She's younger than me."

"I have two sisters," he said. "Both of them younger." He threw back his head and laughed.

"Did you just think of a good joke?"

"Right! You might appreciate it." I smiled expectantly, but he didn't tell it to me. Instead, he asked, "How old is Lizbeth?"

"Eight."

"What's she like? Lizbeth's a cute name. Not short for Elizabeth? Do you two get along? Or is she the proverbial little sister?"

"You ask a lot of questions." I smiled to show I didn't really mind. "She's smart, she's crazy about horses."

"Here's another question for you. Do you think names have anything to do with character? One of my theories of life is that a jerky name means being a jerk. A great name means being a great person. Look at your name. Dani. A boy's name; that's got to influence your life."

61

"My name is Danita; that's not a boy's name. It's a feminine form of Daniel. I'm named for my father."

"Guess what, so am I. Daniel Thomas."

"Your father's name is Daniel, too?"

"Isn't that a chuckle? Thomas is for one of my grandfathers. What's your middle name?"

"Ann, after my great-grandmother."

"Which one? Your mother's grandmother or your father's grandmother? There I go again, asking questions."

"My mother's grandmother," I said.

He stretched out his legs, nodding. "I have a lot of curiosity. I like to know about people. Maybe I should be a journalist instead of a marine biologist. What do you think?"

"You'd be good at it." I stood up and gathered my books. All at once I wanted to get away from him. Maybe it was all the questions, maybe that intense way he had of watching me, then abruptly laughing. Whatever, I was suddenly uncomfortable.

I waved to Laredo and pointed at my watch. "I have to go now," I said to D.T., and I walked quickly away.

"Good-bye, Danita Dani," he called after me. "See you soon, I hope!"

Chapter 13

"Laredo? Hi, it's about time. I thought you'd never answer the phone."

"Dani, talk fast! I don't have much time. Mom'll be home from work in an hour. I've got to have all my homework done by then."

"Why?"

"She doesn't know I'm working, and — "

"Laredo, what does she think you're doing every night when you're not home?"

"It's not *every* night. It's three nights and she's working two of those nights and I get home before her, so that's no problem. As long as I get everything done. Monday night when she's home and I'm working, I'm going to tell her I'm at your house."

"What if she calls up, Laredo? What if my father answers? Or my mother? They'll tell her

63

you're not here, and they'll tell her where you are."

"They know I'm working?"

"Yes."

"You told them?"

"Yes."

"Why did you do that?"

"I didn't *do* it, Laredo. I just happened to mention it."

"I wish you didn't blab everything to your parents, Dani."

"If you didn't want me to say anything, you should have told me. Are we having a fight?"

"I hope not."

"Me, too. I'm sorry I told them, Laredo. I'm sorry because it upsets you. But I don't like you saying *blab* to me. I don't *blab* to people. I don't *blab* to my parents."

"I know, I know, I know! I'm sorry, too. I'm just tired and I'm not thinking about what I'm saying."

"Maybe you're working too much and not sleeping enough. My father says kids our age need a lot of sleep."

"Dani, do you notice you're always quoting your father?"

"I am not."

"You do it all the time. He's your final authority on everything."

"If he happens to be right — "

"How do you know he's right?"

"It makes sense to me. We're growing, our bodies are changing — "

"Making money makes sense to me."

" — and we shouldn't stress them out. When did you get home?"

"About two minutes before you called, Dani. They don't close until nine. Then I have to wait for the bus."

"Did you eat supper there?"

"Pizza and ice cream again. I hope I don't get fat. I got paid tonight. I love making money! As long as I can keep up my schoolwork. . . . If I'm not on the honor roll, my mother will have a fit. . . . Dani, Jon is a funny guy."

"Funny how? Ha ha?"

"No, not that. He never makes a joke. He's quiet. He's actually kind of sweet, but I don't know what I think of him yet. . . . Who was the guy I saw you talking to?"

"You know, the one with red sneakers. D.T. Goodman. Remember? From the video place."

"I thought so! Did he just sit down, or what?"

"I guess he noticed me and . . . he just came around and started talking. He's new here, he comes from California, someplace where Marilyn Monroe lived once."

"Who?"

"Marilyn Monroe!"

"Oh. So what?"

"Nothing. It's just something he told me. I think he's lonely, Laredo. I guess he doesn't know anybody but me yet."

"He's cute, he should make friends fast. . . . How old is he?"

"Nineteen."

"Too old for you, Dani."

"Laredo, all I did was talk to the guy."

"You watch it."

"Watch what?"

"*It*. Yourself. You know what I mean."

"Laredo, he's just a friend. I like *Jon*."

"Uh-huh. Listen, Dani, if you asked your father, he'd tell you the same thing. Nineteen is too old."

"Laredo, you're *hovering*."

"I don't want my girlfriend to do anything foolish."

"Have some trust in me!"

"I do, I do. It's just that sometimes I feel you're so innocent and protected."

"And you're worldly-wise and experienced?"

"All I mean is that your life has been smoother or something than mine. I'm not trying to put anything down on you. I'm not trying to say I know things you don't . . . although I do. I have a better sense of things than you — "

"Laredo, maybe you better hang up and finish your homework."

"Did I make you mad?"

"Ta, my child! Not at all. Not much, anyway. Ta-ta, Laredo. Talk to you tomorrow in school."

Chapter 14

"Dani, how's school going?" my father said. "Are you keeping up the marks?"

"Yes, Dad."

"It's important. Your school record is being made right now."

"I know, Dad." I matched my strides to his. Tonight had been our night to do the dishes together. We had a tradition of going out for a walk around the block as soon as we were done. It was our time together.

I knew what was coming. The *It's not too soon to think about what you're going to do when you graduate college* pep talk. It wasn't that I disagreed with Dad, it was just that I *didn't know* what I was going to do. I wished I did. Laredo knew. Medicine. Lizbeth knew. Veterinary medicine. Even D.T. Goodman knew. Marine biology or journalism. He had *two* choices. I didn't even have one.

"Dad, I've got years before I even graduate high school. I have lots of time."

"It only looks that way now, sweetie. Life goes fast. I don't want you to make the same mistakes I made, letting things slide, letting life happen to you instead of making it happen. Drifting. That's the way I was until I met your mother."

"And then it was love at first sight."

"She was my first love, and I was hers. I went to a movie — "

"And there was Mom ushering — "

"And all I did was watch her, not the movie."

I loved this story; I'd heard it all my life. Was I going to fall in love that way? My thoughts drifted to Jon. If he *had* to have someone else, Shirley was a good choice. *Hypocrite*, a little voice in my head said.

Liking Shirley showed that Jon had good taste. *Really? She's so blonde and showy!*

She was beautiful . . and smart. It meant Jon was the kind of boy who didn't have to be superior to the girl.

Don't be so reasonable. In a minute you'll be saying you don't mind being the lowest of the low backstage.

I liked being part of a crew — one of the gang.

I suppose you love being the bottom rung on the ladder, the one everyone puts their foot on?

"I didn't say that!"

"You didn't say what?" Dad asked.

Had I been talking out loud? I searched my mind for the last thing he had been saying.

Something about Mom and a green scarf on their first date.

"Dad, is that why you still have a favorite green scarf?"

"You got it."

A man was jogging toward us. Just before he reached us, I recognized D.T. Here? *Again?* He came abreast of us, flashed a big smile, and went by.

"I should get back to jogging," Dad said. He patted his belly.

I was sort of in shock. What was D.T. doing here? This wasn't his neighborhood. He was way out of his way! Was it just coincidence or what?

It was hard to believe anything bad about him. I liked his eyes. Brown, soft, gentle. But still . . . could you tell just by looking at a person what sort of character he had? When a horrible crime happened, when some crazed boy shot twelve people and afterward the reporters went to his neighbors, didn't they always say things like, *Oh, he was such a nice, quiet boy! He had such a sweet smile! I would have trusted him with my life!*

I glanced over my shoulder. D.T. was gone. He was always disappearing . . . then popping up again, just when I didn't expect it.

Chapter 15

"Dani! Dani, over here." I put on my glasses to see better. D.T. was standing near a car in front of school.

"What are you doing here?" I said, going up to him.

"I came to see you. How about a ride?"

Don't ever get into a car with a stranger. I could hear my mother's voice.

"Where'd the car come from?" I asked.

"I rented it for the afternoon. I'm not working today. Don't you think it's a great day for a ride?"

"I'm — I'm just going home. I have a lot of homework."

"I bet you're a good student." He had that intense way of gazing at me.

"What were you doing last night?" I said suddenly.

"Last night? Just watching TV in the Y lounge."

"I mean two nights ago," I corrected myself. "When you were jogging on my street."

"Oh, yeah." He smiled. "I was amazed to see you out walking. What a coincidence! Was that your father with you?"

I nodded.

"What do you think the statistical chance of that happening is, Dani? I mean, the two of us meeting like that?"

"I don't know. One in a thousand? Maybe one in a million!" Did he get my meaning? I didn't think it was pure chance he'd been on our street.

D.T. patted the roof of the car. "I miss having wheels. In California, I drove everywhere. Not having a car to jump into when I want to go somewhere feels like having my legs cut off." He held the door open for me. "Come on, I'll drive you home, at least. Dani, what's the matter? It'll be my pleasure! You won't be putting me out of my way."

I hesitated for another moment, then I got in. "Just drive me straight home," I said. "How'd you know I'd be here, anyway? I don't always come out of school so early."

He pulled away from the curb. "I took a chance. You have to take chances in life sometimes if you want something."

And he gave me another one of those intense glances. Was he talking about more than parking in front of our school and waiting for me? What kind of *chance* was that?

"I sold my good old Mustang before I came east," he was saying. "I could have driven cross-country, but my mother didn't want me to. She said she'd worry too much. Now I'm sorry I let her talk me out of it. What do you think, did I do right listening to her?" He put his hand on the back of my neck and gave it a little squeeze.

Maybe I had been stupid to get into the car! I moved closer to the door and put my hand on the handle. Why had he come to school? Why didn't he find a girl his own age to give a ride to?

"Did I tell you I came east with a mission, Dani? I came here to find part of my family."

"Which part?" I glanced at the street sign. "Turn here." If he didn't do what I said, I'd jump out.

"Came to find my father. I never met him. He doesn't even know I'm alive." He laughed briefly.

Was that funny? "Why doesn't he know you're alive?"

He glided to a stop for a red light. "He wasn't around when I was born. He doesn't even know he has a son."

"Why not?"

"Simple. He and my mother weren't married, and he wasn't there when I was born, and she never let him know."

"Oh!"

"Ri-i-i-i-ght," D.T. said, looking at me with a

faint smile. "Now you get it. When my grand-parents found out my mother was pregnant, they picked up and moved away with her. Moved as far as they could go, right across the country. . . . Is this boring you?"

I shook my head. "Were she and your father in love? Why didn't they get married?"

"They were in high school. My grandparents didn't like him. And they were afraid of the disgrace for my mom. You know how it was back then."

"So your grandparents made them break up? That's sad."

D.T. shrugged. "My mother was only sixteen. Her parents were pretty protective of her. She was their only child."

"Sixteen! That's too young to have a baby."

"By the time I was born, she was seventeen, Dani. Anyway, my grandfather says my father took advantage of her."

"Took *advantage* of her?" That was so old-fashioned. "What does your mother say?"

"She says she was too young for everything. She didn't know how to exert her own will then."

Exert her will . . . took advantage of her . . . I wanted to laugh. Was that the way they talked in California?

"If my grandparents hadn't been so worried about what people would say, my mother's whole life might have been different. Mine, too. Once I said that to my grandfather and he blew up. . . . Hey, good buddy, take it easy." D.T.

honked at a car that had cut in front of him. "My grandfather has a temper. I can see why my mother did what he wanted when she was a girl. He's sort of a tyrant."

"Do you have his temper?"

"No way! My mother says I have an easygoing personality. She says it's like my father's personality."

"Well, that's good, isn't it? Does your grandfather know you're here looking for your dad?"

D.T. shook his head slowly. "He knows I'm gone, but not where or why. He thinks I'm goofing off, bumming around the country. He's mad at me. He didn't want me to leave college."

"Couldn't you just tell him the truth?"

"No way," he said. "You'd understand if you knew him." He pulled up in front of my house. "Well, here you are, safe and sound." He gave me a smile, as if he knew what I'd been thinking.

I opened the door and got out. "Thanks for the ride."

"Anybody home?" He looked past me at our house.

"Probably. My mother only works half day today."

"Say, do you think she'd mind if I came in and got a glass of water? I'm really thirsty."

"Oh, uh, sure." I felt a little odd about it, but what else could I say? He followed me up the walk and inside. "Mom?" I called. No answer. "Anybody home? Mom, are you out back?" I went into the kitchen.

"Nice house." D.T. said. "Really nice house."

He was looking at everything, peeking into the living room, looking up the stairs, and glancing into Dad's study. It reminded me of the first time Laredo came to our house. In the kitchen, I looked out the window. The yard was empty. Then I saw the note from Mom on the refrigerator. BACK IN TWENTY MINUTES. WENT TO PICK UP LIZBETH FROM BROWNIES.

I gave D.T. a glass of water. I felt nervous again. If my mother walked in, I didn't know how I'd explain having a stranger in the house. He started to rinse the glass. "No, no, that's all right." I took it from him. "You better go now. I'm not supposed to have people in the house when I'm alone."

"Sure. I understand."

I watched him through the window. He was outside, and I was in. Good. I noticed how he walked, sort of listing to one side, with one shoulder raised more than the other. It was funny, but just then, watching him walk away made me feel, suddenly, as if I didn't have any more doubts about him, as if he were someone I could really trust.

Chapter 16

"I know you're feeling punk because of the job — " I began.

"I'm not," Laredo denied. We were on the way to her house.

"Laredo, it's perfectly normal to feel bad." Her boss had found out how old she was and fired her.

"It doesn't bother me at all, Dani," she said with one breath. And then with the next, "Darn it, I was doing a good job! What difference does it make to them how old I am?"

"Look at it this way, they didn't send you to jail."

"Thank you!" she said. "A real plus. I'm very comforted."

"And he didn't tell your mother, Laredo."

"Another plus," she said.

"And here's a third one for you. You made money."

She smiled when I said that. As soon as we got to her house, the first thing she did was go into her room and open her top bureau drawer. "Look, Dani." She took out a wad of bills and scattered them over the bed, covering it like a green bedspread.

"I'll never have so much money," I said. The only time my parents let me work is weekends, baby-sitting.

Laredo scooped up a handful of bills. "What should I buy? Clothes . . . ? Maybe something for my mother. She wants a toaster oven. I want new dishes. Ours are really grotty. Well, one thing I know I'm going to do is ask a boy out to the movies — "

"You are?"

" — plus, pay for him."

"Why?"

"Because, whoever pays is in charge."

"Why?"

"It's just the way it is. Basic law of the world. That's why boys are always paying for girls. So they can be in charge and snap their fingers and get the girls to do — "

"What?" I said. *"What?"*

"Whatever. But if I pay, I'm the one to snap my fingers!"

"Laredo, that's so cynical. You're saying whoever pays for the other person gets to snap their fingers and do — "

" — whatever. Right."

77

"And whoever gets paid for gets fingers snapped *at* and has done to them — "

" — whatever. . . . Right again," she said.

"But suppose *he* pays, and you don't want him to . . . whatever, because you don't like him that much?"

"Then why am I at the movies with him?"

"You made a mistake. He turned out to be gross and stupid, with dragon breath."

"My bad luck," Laredo said.

"You mean you would still have to — "

"Right. Because he paid."

"That's disgusting! That's not free will. I'm never going to . . . whatever we're talking about, just because someone paid for a dumb movie for me."

"Then you better pay for your own dumb movies."

"Believe me, I will, Laredo."

"Who are you going with?"

"I'm not going with anyone, Laredo. You're the one who's going. What boy are you going to ask?"

"I haven't made up my mind yet. Any suggestions?"

"Just do not ask Ronnie or Davis Buck, or I might never speak to you again."

"Oh, them," she snickered. "Don't worry, I wouldn't. That was pure desperation that day I let them hang around me in the gym."

"Why don't you ask Geo?"

"No, Dani, he's my phone friend."

"So?"

"It wouldn't work, because whoever I choose — I've got it all planned out — I go up to him, tap him on the shoulder, and say, 'You're invited to a movie, paid for by me!' "

"So tap Geo on the shoulder."

"Dani, how do I tap him on the shoulder over the phone?"

"Give me two minutes and I'll figure it out," I said.

Laredo laughed and shuffled her money together like a pack of cards. "Let's get something to eat." We went into the kitchen and made fruit-and-ice cream shakes. "Why don't we double date?" she said. "You ask someone to the movies, too."

"No. I can't do that."

"Yes, you can. I want you to have a date. You're so cute, I can't understand why the guys aren't flocking to your door — "

"Maybe they don't know my address."

"Dani, be serious. It's about time you had your first date. I bet even your father wouldn't mind."

"I wouldn't count on that," I said, tipping up my glass. But what I was thinking was that nobody was calling me. Nobody was asking me to go to a movie. Nobody was asking me to go anywhere.

But I didn't take Laredo and her plans into account.

Chapter 17

"Dani, hi. Laredo here. What are you doing?"

"Not much. Reading. How about you?"

"Oh, you'll see. You'll see what I've been up to. Where are you, Dani, in the kitchen?"

"Yes."

"Who else is there?"

"No one. My parents went out. Lizbeth's watching TV."

"Excellent. Sit down, I have something to tell you. I did something for you."

"Why do I have to sit down?"

"Take the phone and sit down, Dani, so you don't fall down. I called Jon."

"What?"

"You heard me. I called Jon Haberle and invited him to a movie."

"You want to tell me that again?"

"I. Called. Jon. And. I invited. Him. To. A. Movie."

"Why?"

"I did it for you."

"Am I missing something here, Laredo? I thought you said *you* invited him to a movie. How is that supposed to benefit me?"

"Open your ears. Listen. And you will understand. I called Jon, and this is what I said. 'Hi, is this Jon?' He said, 'Yes.' I said. 'Hi-i-i-i! This is Dani Merritt.' "

"You didn't say that."

"I did."

"Laredo, you didn't say it."

"I did."

"Laredo, tell me you didn't say, 'This is Dani Merritt.' "

"Dani, I said it."

"Laredo! What are you telling me?"

"Dani, what I am telling you is that I did a really good thing for you. Now I'm going to tell you again. Very slowly. I called Jon Haberle. *The* Jon Haberle. Angel boy. Blond boy. And I said . . . 'Hi!' And he said, 'Hi.' And I said, 'This is Dani Merritt.' And he said, 'Oh, hi, Dani,' And I said, 'Hi, Jon.' "

"How many times did you say hi, for god's sake!"

"Easy, girl, easy."

"Laredo!"

"To continue, Dani, I next said . . . 'Jon, I was wondering . . . would you like to go to a movie with me Friday night?' "

"This is a joke. This is supposed to be funny, right? Okay, I'm going to laugh. Ha ha. Now the joke is over. Right?"

"Wrong. It's not April Fools' Day, Dani. It's not even Halloween yet. I'm serious. Consider this an early birthday present. I swear to you, this is what I did. I just hung up with Jon. You could call him up now and ask him."

"I will not!"

"Well, you've got a date with him Friday. This is Tuesday. Wednesday, Thursday, then comes Friday, and you and Jon will be at the movies together. . . . Hello? Are you there?"

"I can't believe this. I don't want to believe this. How could you do a thing like this to me? What got into you? What happened to your brains?"

"Jeeze, Dani, I thought they were working overtime."

"You did this behind my back, Laredo! You didn't even ask me."

"What if I had? What would you have said?"

"I would have said what any normal person would say. Forget it! No, you can't do it! No! No way!"

"That's what I thought. That's why I didn't ask you."

"Laredo, you really did it? You actually called Jon?"

"Yes."

"But what were you thinking of? What was going through your mind? I thought you were smart. How can you be a doctor if you're not a smart person?"

"I am a very smart person and getting smarter. This was not a dumb thing, Dani. The only dumb thing is how you're reacting."

"I beg your pardon? Hello? My reaction is dumb? My best friend goes crazy, impersonates me behind my back, and I'm dumb to be mad?"

"I wanted to do something nice for you."

"Then you should have stuffed a tablecloth in your mouth."

"Thank you so much. Do you want to know how it happened?"

"I thought I just heard."

"I mean *why* it happened."

"No! But I guess I'm going to hear, anyway."

"First I called Geo. You know who Geo is?"

"Yes, I know who Geo is. Naturally, I know who Geo is! Geo is your phone friend. What does Geo have to do with any of this?"

"You haven't met Geo."

"Right! Neither have you."

"Exactly the point. I called Geo, and we were talking as usual about this and that and everything, and we were saying how great it was that we were friends, even though we'd only talked to each other on the phone. And then I said, 'Well, Geo, maybe it's time we met.' You remember how he and I met last summer, Dani, when he called the wrong number, and — "

"I know the story. I know the whole story, Laredo. Thank you very much. You can skip it."

"Calm down. I want to tell this my own way."

"Don't talk to me like I'm a dog, Laredo. Woof woof! I'm going to hang up. You've got a real attitude tonight."

"*I've* got a real attitude? Dani, hello! Planet Earth is calling. We're talking about Geo. Okay? So I said, 'Geo, let's go out to a movie or something, I'll pay!' "

"Ha! I told you to ask Geo, and you said you wouldn't."

"Well, I decided you were right, Dani. I decided on the spur of the moment. And I'm glad I did. Geo was so enthusiastic! He said, 'Great! I've been waiting for you to say that.' I said, 'What, that I'd pay for your movie?' I was teasing, but then he got so embarrassed. He kept apologizing. 'No, no, I don't mean about paying! About us meeting.' He was *very* cute."

"What does this have to do with Jon?"

"Well, I got to thinking. Geo is so nice on the phone, but what if he's different in person? What if he turns out to be a big disappointment? What if he's this prematurely bald, shrimpy guy?"

"He could be cross-eyed, knock-kneed, and bowlegged, Laredo. And have dragon breath, besides."

"Right. So this is where you and Jon come in."

"You mean you and Jon."

"No, I mean YOU and Jon. Because, we're all going to go to the same movie. Geo and me. You and Jon. Double date."

"Laredo, point of information. I'm not going

to a movie with Jon. I'm not going anywhere with Jon, because I wasn't asked."

"You asked him. And he accepted."

"No! I didn't ask Jon anything!"

"Dani, when you think about this in a calm frame of mind, you're going to realize I did a selfless act for you. You're going to be happy I'm your friend and did this. You're going to be thanking me for a long, long time."

"Laredo, I can hardly make sense out of this. I'm so — so — "

" — surprised?"

"That hardly says it! How about astonished? Amazed. Dazed! No, when you get down to it, Laredo I'm *dead*. D-E-A-D. I'm supposed to be going out with Jon, and I've never said more than three words to him, and they were all about ice cream."

"Don't you worry about a thing, Dani. I'll be right there with you the whole evening. Same movie, remember?"

"Did you tell him it was going to be a double date, when you called up and impersonated me?"

"I didn't think it was necessary. I didn't want to confuse the situation."

"Thoughtful."

"Sarcasm will not get you out of this. Here's the scenario. On Friday night — "

"The scenario? Are we in a movie, Laredo? Have you totally lost touch with reality?"

" — you come to my house, and we go to the theater together. Geo shows up. Hello, hello. I introduce you. We both look him over. Meanwhile, we're waiting for Jon. Now, what if Geo turns out to be a dog? This is where you'll see how brilliant my plan is. Because you will then save my life by sticking close to me, so I won't be stuck alone with Geo. Maybe it sounds heartless — "

"I didn't say it, you did."

" — but I'm just trying to be more realistic than I usually am. Not build castles in the air. Anyway, the other part of the brilliant plan is that if you're having any problems talking to Jon, or anything, I save *your* life by being there."

"Thank you, Laredo! I can't tell you how much I appreciate your concern. It's really touching! What would I do without you?"

"Dani, when did you get so sarcastic? Just remember this, I did it for you. By calling Jon, I got you over what could be the hardest moment of your life. I know you. Without me, you could be lurking behind curtains for the rest of your life."

"Maybe I don't have that much longer to live. I might just kill myself before I have to go to school tomorrow morning and face Jon."

Chapter 18

The next day was a total day of dread.

I didn't want to see Jon.

What would I say? What *could* I say? And how would I act? Guilty? Pleased? Panicked?

All morning I slunk through the halls, avoiding every place I'd ever seen him.

I saw him, anyway, later in the afternoon, talking to some other guys. They were laughing and pounding each other the way boys do, as if they know some wild, funny, energetic secret. I always wonder what it is they say to make each other laugh like that.

But that day I knew. They were talking about me. Me and "my" phone call. Oh, yes. What else could they be laughing about except Danita Merritt, an eighth-grader who had the total brassy nerve to ask a junior boy for a date!

My face blazed, my neck was sweating. Was I sick? Feverish? Was I going to die? That wouldn't be so bad, as long as I passed away quickly and painlessly, and before Friday night.

Chapter 19

I was on my way upstairs to bed when the phone rang. "I'll get it up here," I called.

"No, Dad's got it," Mom answered.

Which meant I had no reason to pick up the phone in my parents' room. I know why I went in there — to borrow one of Mom's shirts for school tomorrow. But why did I pick up the phone? Why did I eavesdrop? I don't do that. I hadn't done it for years, not since I was Lizbeth's age. It was almost as if I knew something.

First I heard Dad. "Well, who are you, exactly? I don't understand. Could you tell me — "

"Mr. Merritt, I just want to meet you and talk to you," the other person said. "I have something to tell you. I think it'll be interesting to you."

"Is this a business call?"

89

"Well, yes and no. I'll tell you everything when we meet."

That was when I recognized D.T.'s voice.

"I don't do business this way," Dad said. "If you want to meet me, Mr., uh — you know you didn't identify yourself . . ."

"But that's part of what I'll tell — " D.T. began.

Dad cut him off. "Why don't you call the print shop tomorrow and ask my receptionist for an appointment? Good-bye." He hung up.

I went back to my room. I couldn't fall asleep. The phone conversation kept replaying in my mind like a tape. *I'll tell you everything . . . I just want to meet you and talk to you . . . it'll be interesting to you . . . I promise . . .*

Should I tell Dad about D.T.? What would I tell him, though? I didn't know anything about D.T., really, just that he was from California, and he was here on a "mission." Wasn't that the word he'd used? A mission. To find his father. What did Dad have to do with that? Maybe D.T. thought my father had known his father years ago.

I turned over and pushed my pillow into a soft lump the way I liked it. Maybe D.T. had gotten that idea because I'd told him Dad had grown up in Menands, the same place where D.T.'s mother and father had come from. That made sense. But why didn't he just say it to Dad? Why be so mysterious? Oh, I knew! That was D.T. He was so dramatic; he had that intense way of looking at you and waiting to see your reaction, just staring you straight in the face. I tried to imagine D.T. and Dad meeting. I wondered if Dad would like him.

Oh, well, I decided finally, if D.T. wanted to go for Dad, why not? Let him do it! If he was lucky enough to get an appointment with Dad during his working hours, more power to him. I only wished I could be there, a fly on the wall, watching it all.

Chapter 20

Laredo and I were eating lunch when Jon stopped at our table, tapped me on the shoulder, and said, "Dani? I guess we're going to a movie tonight."

"Yeah." My eyes kept shutting, the way they do when you stare up into the sun.

"Well, how do we do this? Where do we meet? We didn't talk about that the other night."

"There. At the movie theater," I got out.

"I guess it would help if you told me which one."

This was so embarrassing. I hated Laredo. She was just sitting there, chewing her sandwich and looking smug. I said the name of the theater. "Seven o'clock; the movie begins at seven."

"See you then." He walked away.

I let out my breath. "This is not going to work," I said. "This is terrible. I can't talk to him. He doesn't want to go out with me — he's just too nice to say it. Anyway, he's going with Shirley."

"Dani, if he was going with her, why would he go out with you?"

"I don't know. That's the question. Why?!"

"Look on the bright side," Laredo urged. "You're going to the movies with Jon Haberle! If somebody told you that you HAD to ask a boy to the movies, that it was a test or something, who would you have asked?"

"I don't know. Nobody."

"Come on," she said patiently. "It's a test. You have to take it. Who would you have wanted to ask?"

"Jon . . ." I mumbled.

"So there you are!"

"So there I am, where?"

"So there you are with me having picked the right person. Dani, no insult meant, but you know you would never have had the nerve to do for yourself what I did for you."

"You're right."

"Admit I did something valuable for you. Like a boost over a fence you've wanted to climb."

"Who says I wanted to climb the fence? I never said a word to you, Laredo — "

"Shhh! Dani, will you relax?! Relax and be yourself, just be yourself, so Jon can see what a great person you are."

"Laredo, I'm less relaxed than I've ever been in my entire life. Tomorrow night is going to be a disaster."

"Tonight," Laredo said. "Tonight's the night."

"Oh, help." I buried my head in my arms.

Chapter 21

I think what I did after school was mainly to get my mind off my date with Jon. I went over to the Springfield Mall to look for D.T. I was going to ask him why he'd called my father. It was drizzling. I walked fast, heating up, my face and hair getting wet. I could hear my father's voice. *Dani, you could have caught a bad cold!*

I ran and walked, ran and walked. I felt strong, too strong to catch a cold. Was I strong enough to catch something else? Someone else? Catch D.T. in his little scheme, or whatever it was? I laughed. I suddenly felt really good. I'd find out what he was up to, and then I'd go to Dad and say, *Look, Dad, this is what that phone call the other night was all about. I found out about it for you. Me, your daughter Dani, the one you're always hovering over, the one you think can't chew gum and take ten deep breaths at the same time!*

It didn't occur to me that D.T. might not be at You Can Be a Star, Too. I just barged on ahead, happily planning to confront him. But when I got there and rang the bell on the counter, a boy I'd never seen before came out from the back.

"Is D.T. here?" I asked.

"D.T.?" the boy said, as if I were speaking Russian.

"He works here."

"Who?"

"D.T. Goodman."

"Goodman?" he said doubtfully.

Just then, a man holding a tiny girl by the hand came in. The man had a snouty nose, thin lips, stiff whiskers sticking out from each side of his face. "My daughter wants to be a star!" he said. He looked like a turtle, and the girl looked like a fish — a silvery face with green eyes.

The boy rang a bell, and the woman who'd helped Laredo came out. She was wearing the same silver dress.

"My daughter wants to be a star!" the man said.

The woman in the silver dress smiled at the tiny girl. "You've come to the right place." She opened the door and took them in back.

"I'm looking for *D.T. Goodman*," I started again. I put my hand up to indicate his height. "Red sneakers. A ponytail."

"Ponytail?"

Was I still speaking Russian? "D.T. Good-man," I said again.

"He works here," the boy admitted.

"Is he here? I'd like to see him."

"Do you want to make a video?"

"No. I came to see D.T. It's business," I added.

"Business?" We were back to foreign languages.

"Business," I said, standing up straighter.

"He's on his break now."

I left and walked around the mall, looking into this place and that for D.T., but being careful not to go anywhere near Ice Dreams. I didn't want to even *think* about Jon right now.

I found D.T. sitting at the counter in a sandwich shop. I went in and sat down next to him. He swiveled around. "Dani!"

"D.T., I want to ask you something. Why'd you phone my father?"

"What?"

"You called our house the other day."

"How do you know that?"

"I picked up the phone, and I recognized your voice."

He put down his sandwich and looked at me. "I guess I might as well tell you, though this is a weird place to do it."

"Tell me what?"

He kind of coughed and cleared his throat. "Don't you think it's, uh, interesting that we have the same name?"

Why was he talking about our names? "We don't have the same name, D.T. Didn't we have this conversation once before? Your name is Daniel. My name is Danita."

"Masculine and feminine forms of the same name. Or let me put it this way. We're both named for our fathers. Your father is Daniel, my father is Daniel."

"I know, I know. We talked about that, too. Lots of people are named for their fathers. D.T., do you think my father knew your father in high school? I was wondering what you wanted to talk to Dad about. And I remembered you said your mom and dad went to high school in Menands, the same as my father, so it just suddenly clicked — "

"Dani." He put his hand over mine. "Slow down. Wait a second. Listen to me."

"Your father and my father might have been friends."

"Dani." His voice was quiet. "Dani, I don't know any way to say this except to say it. I'm your brother."

I wanted to smile, felt my lips twitching.

"I'm your brother," he said again. "Your father and my father are the same person."

On the wall in front of me was a sign. IN CASE WE TRUST. I kept reading it.

"That's why we have the same names. I mean related names. Daniel and Danita. We're both named for him."

"Daniel and Danita," I said. "Sounds like a law firm or a department store, doesn't it," I joked.

"I called the other night so I could make an

appointment to see him. I didn't want to just dump it all on him over the phone. I don't want him to think I'm some punk kid. I want him to meet me. I want him to know me."

I squinted at the sign. IN CASE WE TRUST . . . In case of what? Emergency? What if it said, IN TRUST WE CASE? Would that make more sense? I picked up a glass of water and drank. Suddenly it all came clear to me. D.T. was searching for his father. He'd met me by chance, but when he found out the coincidence of our names, he'd snapped onto it like a dog with a bone, decided that our names proved *my* father was *his* father. Logical, in a crazy sort of way.

"Your father is the one my grandparents didn't like," D.T. said.

I almost shook my finger in his face. That proved how off base he was. Everyone liked Daniel Merritt. Everyone!

"So what do you think?" he said. "You want to say anything? Say *something*, Dani. I thought you'd be glad."

Just then, I realized I was reading the sign wrong. It was IN CASH WE TRUST.

"Dani, would you look at me? Aren't you going to say anything?"

Sure I'll say something. You're crazy, D.T. I'm sorry to say it, because you're a nice guy, but this is out and out nuts. It's something you made up to make yourself feel better. I know you want to find your father, but you can't just pick one out of thin air.

"Remember, I told you my mom told me the whole story, Dani? Ever since then, I wanted to

99

meet him. She told me when I was thirteen. Your age."

"I'm almost fourteen," I said.

D.T. laughed. "Dani, that's not the point. Are you paying attention?"

"Don't talk to me like that." I felt irritable suddenly. My whole good mood had evaporated. "If this is true, how come your name isn't Merritt?"

"Goodman is my mother's name. . . . Dani, come on, you can believe me; it's not like the world just split apart."

My chest was tight and heavy inside. I coughed, trying to clear something out. Maybe I was getting a cold. Maybe it *had* been stupid to run in the rain and get overheated. Maybe I should go home and get into bed and forget D.T., forget the movies and Jon, forget everything! Just get into bed and let my mother bring me tea and toast on a tray.

"Dani, I'm not blaming him. I'm not here to get anything from him. That's not what you think, is it?"

"Were you the wrong numbers?" I said suddenly, remembering all the phone calls. "Someone kept calling and saying it was a wrong number and asking questions about — it was you, wasn't it?"

D.T. nodded.

"That was sneaky, D.T.! You got me to talk and say things!"

He looked hurt. "I didn't think you'd react

100

this way. I called to talk to him, but then you answered."

"And you followed me, didn't you!? In the mall, you bumped right into me; you must have been following me."

"That was a coincidence. Like you and your girlfriend coming to Star. That was pretty funny. When I saw you walking in that day, I thought, Wow, this really is fate!"

"What about being across the street from our house? And how about last week when I saw you jogging on our street? That wasn't *fate*, that was you!"

"Last week, when you were with him?"

"Yes, I was with my father. Why didn't you stop and say something to us? That was a perfect opportunity, wasn't it?"

"I chickened out." D.T. made a face. "I wanted to see him so much, and there he was, and then I just kept going." He shrugged. "I admit it, I got scared. Maybe I shouldn't have done things the way I did, Dani. But I didn't mean anything wrong by it." He stood up and put money down on the counter. "I want to talk some more, but I should get back to work."

I sat there. "You didn't have to come here," I said. "All the way across the country — what good is it?"

He gave me another hurt look. "Dani, doesn't it mean anything to you that I'm your brother?"

"Half brother," I said. "*If* you are."

"I am."

101

"Anybody could just say what you're saying, D.T."

"Maybe. But I'm telling the truth. Why are you so upset?"

"Because it's my father," I almost shouted at him. "You're saying things about my father!" Tears rushed into my eyes.

"My mother said I shouldn't push it." D.T. sat down again. "She didn't want me to come. She said I didn't know what I'd find. But I'm stubborn. It's not a whim that I'm here! I left school. I left my friends. I'm working at a dinky job, I'm living in a dinky room."

I pressed a napkin against my lips.

He took a picture from his wallet. "This is my mother, Dani." It showed D.T. — younger, wearing baggy, flowered shorts and holding a baseball glove, standing next to a tall woman in a pink dress with her arm around his shoulders. They were both smiling.

I thought about the stories I'd heard all my life about my birth. How I'd been a preemie, so tiny, no bigger than a thumbnail, kept in an isolette, how even when they took me home I'd been small enough to fit into my father's palm. I'd been first. That's what I'd always thought. First daughter. Firstborn.

"How much did you weigh when you were born?" I said.

"Nine pounds. Why?"

"I don't know, I just wondered. I was a preemie."

"My mother says all she did was eat while she was pregnant. And cry."

"Nine pounds? I weighed less than a loaf of bread."

He put the picture back into his wallet. "I want to talk to you some more, Dani. When can we talk?"

I didn't answer him. I jumped off the stool and walked out, almost ran down the broad mall corridor. But then, just before the door, I turned and looked back and saw D.T. starting down the stairs. And I noticed again that funny way he had of sort of listing to one side when he walked. *My brother* . . . Was he really my father's son? Was he really my brother?

Chapter 22

"I hope Geo's skinny," Laredo said for about the fourth time since we'd entered the lobby of the movie theater. People kept coming in, pushing through the doors, meeting and greeting each other. "I hope he turns out to be one of those bony, romantic types with a lot of cheekbone. Maybe a dimple in his chin."

"Uh-huh."

"You're quiet tonight."

"I am?"

"Don't worry about Jon. You're going to do fine, Dani!"

I wasn't worrying about Jon. He hardly even seemed real to me just then. D.T., though — *he* was real. What if I said to Laredo, *I have a brother. . . . You think it's only coincidence D.T. and I have*

104

almost the same first names? Would Laredo laugh and tell me I had a great imagination?

"Dani, look!" She clutched my arm. A tall, skinny, good-looking guy had just walked in. "That's him." She gave him a big smile, and he came right over to us. "Geo?" she said.

"No, it's Andy," he said. "Will that do?"

"Sorry, wrong number," Laredo said. The boy laughed and walked away.

A moment later I noticed a husky boy wearing a blue nylon jacket. He had a round face with bright red cheeks. His hair was cut short and straight, and he wore nerdy black sneakers. He was standing in the middle of the lobby, looking sort of lost.

"Laredo," I said, "over there. That's him. That's Geo."

"No," she said. "No, no, no. Definitely not."

"Yes. I have an instinct. It's him. Want me to ask?" I walked over to him. "Geo?"

"Laredo? Great!" He shook my hand excitedly.

His hand was like a nice, hot roll. I liked him right away. He was the kind of boy you feel comfortable with, a sort of Saint Bernard boy, the kind that would make a fine brother.

The moment I thought it, my heart pumped crazily. Was D.T. my brother or wasn't he? Why didn't I just *know*? Why did I have the instinct to pick out Geo from the whole crowd in the lobby and yet not be sure about D.T.? If he was my brother, wouldn't I feel something special, something more than just friendship for him?

105

Geo was still holding my hand. "Geo, I'm Dani Merritt," I said. "I'm Laredo's friend. That's her over there."

"Dani, I know about you! Laredo talks about you all the time." He bounded over to Laredo, and they started shaking hands. "Laredo, do I look the way you expected?" he asked.

She coughed. "Oh, I didn't have too much of a fixed image, Geo."

Geo went off to buy popcorn. Laredo said that maybe the two of them ought to go in and get seats for all of us. "And leave me out here alone?" I said.

"Look at the crowd, Dani. If we don't go in, you and Jon might not even get seats."

I watched her and Geo disappear. The lobby emptied out. Suddenly a girl with a long black braid came rushing in, ran up to a boy — the only other person waiting, besides me — and kissed him on the mouth.

What if Jon wanted to kiss me? Was there some sort of a signal I should be watching for? In the movies, you could tell when people wanted to kiss by the way they swayed toward each other with their lips puckered up and quivering. It always sent chills through my stomach. But I'd never thought before about when to sway or who swayed first.

The usher closed the doors to the theater. Now, nobody was in the lobby except me and the woman behind the popcorn counter.

"Miss, the movie's started."

"I'm waiting for a friend."

Was he a friend? He was hardly even an acquaintance. Was waiting for him silly? How did I know he'd even show up? I didn't. Maybe it was all a big joke to him. Maybe he'd stopped by our table in the cafeteria just to tease me. What if his boyfriends had been watching? Did Shirley know about this, too? What if they'd all cooked up a scheme to teach me a lesson, to put me in my place, to make me remember I was the bottom rung on the ladder?

My face was hot. *Go in*, I told myself. *You don't have to stand here and wait for him. You've waited long enough.*

I didn't move. Jon had said he'd meet me here, and I was going to wait until he did, even if it meant waiting all night. I remembered D.T. saying he was stubborn. Maybe I was, too. Did that make us siblings? Two stubborn people?

Then Jon came in. He pushed through the doors swiftly, like the girl with the black braid, only he didn't rush up and kiss me. Instead, he slowed down and stared. "Dani?" he said.

Who did he expect?

"You're still here," he said.

No kidding.

"I'm late because my mother needed the car tonight, so she had to drive me, and then we had a flat tire."

Flat tire? The oldest excuse in the world! Why didn't he tell the truth, just say he didn't want to come? Probably his mother'd had to push him out the door.

"Flat as a pancake," he said. "Look at this."

He held out his hands for inspection. They didn't look so awful. He could have rubbed that little bit of dirt on them himself.

We went into the theater. It was packed and dark. I didn't know where Laredo was. Jon and I sat down in the back row. "Do you know what's going on?" he whispered. On the screen, a girl behind a counter was selling a record to a boy. "Maybe we can figure it out together," he said, and he squeezed my hand.

I shivered. Maybe he really did have a flat tire.

I think the movie was good, but I'm not sure. Half the time Jon's arm was over the back of my seat. Between that and thinking of D.T., I had trouble concentrating.

When the lights came on, Jon said, "So, that's that." It was like brushing his hands off, or flicking away an insect. Did that mean he'd done his duty and now he could leave?

I looked around for Laredo and saw her and Geo way down toward the front.

Jon checked his watch. "My mother will be here in about twenty minutes." He had a precise way of talking that I hadn't noticed before. Well, how could I? I still hadn't had more than five sentences worth of conversation with him.

"She'll drive you home, Dani, but we do have time for an ice cream before she gets here. Yes?"

"Sure, but — " I pointed to Laredo. "My girl-friend — I'm sleeping over at her house." I went down the aisle to meet Laredo.

Geo said, "Dani!" like we were old friends, and he hugged me.

"How's it going?" Laredo said.

"Pretty good. How about you?"

"Great!"

I told Laredo about Jon's mother taking me home. "Geo and I are walking," she said. So that was *that*.

Jon and I went across the street to Westie's. Jon studied the menu for a long time. "You know me and ice cream," he said. So he did remember me coming into Ice Dreams! He ordered a strawberry banana split, and I ordered a dish of peach ice cream.

"You're a nice girl, Dani," Jon said.

"I am?" I could feel a silly smile spreading across my face. Why didn't I just say thank you in a dignified way?

The waitress brought the ice cream. Jon ate a crescent of banana. "It was nice of you to ask me to the movie. I almost didn't accept, Dani, but you were very persuasive."

"I was?"

"You seemed sure of yourself."

"I did?"

"I was a little surprised because I didn't, don't, have that impression of you. But as I said, you persuaded me. And it was a good movie. And another thing, you waited for me, even though I was late. A lot of girls would have gotten mad."

Why was he telling me how nice I was? He was practically patting me on the head. I no sooner thought it than he did it. He leaned toward me, patted me on the head, and said, "I want to tell you something . . . I think I should tell you this."

Oh, no. I didn't want to hear it. I knew what was coming. My instincts clicked into place.

"I hope you don't take this the wrong way, but Shirley Larkin and — you know Shirley, don't you?"

I nodded. "Greasepaint."

"Well, the deal is that Shirley and I are thinking seriously about going together."

"Going together?" I repeated faintly.

"And we talked about you. And me going out with you."

Oh, *no.* I concentrated on taking tiny bites of the cold ice cream.

"We're seriously thinking of going steady," he said again. "We don't want you to get the wrong idea, that I'm, uh, boyfriend material."

"Boyfriend material," I echoed.

He leaned across the table, as if he were going to pat me on the head again.

I sat back, out of reach. "I don't have the wrong idea," I said. A definite Major Fib. "I don't think going steady is a good idea, though. I think we're too young to go steady."

I got so unnerved when I heard what I'd said — *we're* too young — that I knocked over my dish of ice cream.

"Well, I wasn't talking about you," he said. "You're too young, I agree."

I started scooping up blobs of melting peach

ice cream with my fingers and dumping them back into the dish.

"You're not going to eat that, are you?" he said.

"Maybe I am!" Why did I say that? I seemed to be completely out of control. "What I meant before was that people in our peer group are too immature to go steady." Did I say that? *Peer group? Immature?* "Maybe I don't know as much as you, but that's my opinion. Besides, you're not that much older than me."

"I'm seventeen," he said.

"I'm almost fourteen."

"At your age, I was a lot different. I definitely didn't know much."

An answer was right there on the tip of my tongue. *If you know so much now, why didn't you tell me all this before you went to the movies with me?* I grabbed a napkin and started wiping the table.

"The waitress will clean that up," Jon said, as if he'd been in a thousand different restaurants and a thousand different situations in his seventeen long years of life.

I dropped the mess of napkins on top of the ice cream. Maybe I would have a heart attack now and be spared further humiliation. D.T. crept into my mind. *He* never patronized me. But how could I compare him and Jon? Jon was a romance, a crush, a disappointment of the heart! D.T. was . . . well, what *was* he? A man with a mission. My brother. My maybe brother.

"You'll see things differently, when you're

over being thirteen," Jon was saying.

Over being thirteen? Did he think it was a disease?

"I guess we should go," he said, standing up.

When his mother came, Jon got right in the front seat next to her. The back seat for me. Was my heart broken? *Yes.* No! I couldn't decide.

Mrs. Haberle pulled up in front of Laredo's house, and I stuck out my hand to Jon. "I enjoyed the evening," I said. "And the talk. And I stick to what I said before," I went on fast, before I lost my nerve. "You're too young to go steady."

Boom! I was out of the car. I was gone. Jon was history.

Chapter 23

"Geo and I got along like bread and butter," Laredo said, leaning on her elbow in the bed. "Or maybe like coffee and cake. I really think he likes me."

"*Likes* you, or just . . . likes you?" I said from the floor. I zipped the sleeping bag up a bit higher.

"*Likes* me."

"Oh!"

"He was very romantic during the movie . . . and afterward. He's definitely a decent kisser."

"You kissed him? Isn't that deceptive?"

"Deceptive? Dani, why?"

"Because you like him, but you don't *like* him."

"Well . . . to be honest, you're right. I don't know how much I *like* him. He's very cute,

113

though . . . in a sort of chunky way. Anyway, he needs practice kissing."

"So you were being kind, giving him a helping hand — I mean, mouth?"

"That's the idea. My favorite charity. My contribution to a good cause." She fell back, laughing. "I'm all heart! Did Jon kiss you? Did you kiss him?"

"What was I supposed to do, lean over the front seat and kiss him under his mom's nose? Anyway. I told you what he said about him and Shirley."

"It's probably just as well you didn't try anything. I bet ice cubes form on *his* lips when he kisses! Why did he have to tell you about Shirley Larkin? Just to make sure your heart was completely broken? What I can't understand is why, when you called him — "

"Laredo! *I* didn't call Jon."

" — why, when a girl saying she was Dani Merritt called and asked him to go out, he agreed. I mean if he knew he was going steady with another girl — "

"He didn't say definitely. He said it was in the serious considering stage."

"You're too kind. How did you feel when he told you about him and Shirley talking about you? I think that's horrible! That's so mean."

"That's the way I felt, horrible."

"He's a brute. A monster from the deep! Did he have a mean, sadistic smile on his face when he told you?"

"Not exactly. More of a patronizing grin."

"Well, you told him something, anyway! Did you really say he was too young to go steady?"

"Uh-huh."

"And you said it twice. I'm proud of you." She pounded the pillow. "My girlfriend is nervy!"

The next day I went home around noon. I got there just in time to help Mom finish the big Saturday house cleaning. "You want to vacuum upstairs, sweetie?" she said. She was wearing jeans, an old shirt of my father's, and a red scarf tied around her forehead.

"Vacuuming is my greatest desire, Mom." I started toward the stairs, hauling the cleaner after me.

The phone rang. "Oh, that reminds me," Mom said, as she picked it up, "you had a call last night from a boy."

"A boy!" Had Jon had a change of heart? "Who?"

"Hello. Merritts'," Mom said into the phone. She pointed to the message pad on the table, and I peered over her shoulder. "Friday eve.," she'd scribbled. "D.T. wants to talk to Dani. Call him."

Chapter 24

"Will you help me out, Dani?" D.T. said.

I pulled the long cord on the phone and walked around the kitchen, looking out the window into the backyard. "I don't know."

"I could do it on my own, but it would be better if you were there."

Dad was gathering branches that had blown down from the willow in a rainstorm last week. "You just want to talk to my father?"

"*Our* . . . father," D.T. said softly.

I remembered Laredo saying, *My girlfriend is nervy!* Was I, really? I didn't think so. If I was *really* nervy, I'd demand proof from D.T. *Show me something official . . . prove my father is your father . . .*

"Dani, I just want to sit down with him some-

116

where and talk, someplace neutral. Neutral territory."

"Sounds like war, D.T. Like two enemies coming together."

"I just mean somewhere we can talk where everybody will be comfortable. This is going to be a shock to him. Here's this nineteen-year-old son he doesn't even know he has. . . ."

Dad noticed me looking out the window and did a little pantomime of picking up branches, then wiping sweat off his forehead.

"With you there, it'll be easier for everybody," D.T. was saying.

"Easier for you . . ."

"You think I'm selfish? I'm not being purely selfish. It'll be easier for him, too. Maybe I should write him a letter, first. Explain everything. What do you think?"

"If you want to . . ."

"But that's dragging it out again. Isn't it better if I do this face to face? I'll never get things right in a letter. He can't see me in a letter. He won't know what kind of person I am. That's why I thought the three of us would be the best thing."

I didn't know what to say. I felt so confused. I tried to imagine D.T. and me in Dad's office. His old oak desk and the two chairs would be piled high with papers, orders, and samples. Dad's face would light up when he saw me. He'd clean the mess off the chairs, the way he always did when I came to visit, and he'd ask if I wanted a soft drink. Then he'd notice D.T.

He'd be surprised to see me with someone so

much older. A boy. So maybe he wouldn't be smiling. I'd say, *Dad, I want you to meet D.T.* and then I'd say quickly, *He says he's your son . . .* Dad would look from me to D.T., puzzled. But why would I say anything? It was D.T.'s story. He was the one who had to talk.

"Dani, are you there?" D.T. said.

"Yes . . ." I wiped a water spot off the window.

Part of me really wanted to help D.T. But another part of me kept stubbornly thinking, *Where's the proof?*

Dad was walking down toward the back of the yard now with a load of branches.

"I can feel that you're reluctant, Dani. Listen, I can do it myself. I don't want to pressure you."

I was watching Dad, the way he was walking, the way he held his shoulders, one higher and further forward than the other.

"I'll figure it out," D.T. said. "It's my problem."

"Yes," I said. But I was thinking that at last I knew who D.T.'s odd way of walking reminded me of, at last I knew who the other person was who had that same sideways list.

Chapter 25

"What if he doesn't come?" I said, peering in the window of Cosmo's. Two aisles of red leather booths, a long counter, and a lot of men in black vests running around serving food and coffee.

"D.T.'s going to come," Laredo said. I'd told her everything about him. She'd listened calmly and then commented, "Well that's great, now you have a brother, too." As if there were no questions at all. "Why wouldn't he show up?" she said. "It's his meeting."

"No, I mean my *father*."

"Don't be paranoid." She plucked my hand off her arm. "Ugh, you're sweating like a pig."

"Pigs don't sweat, Laredo. They don't have a natural cooling system like we do. That's why they roll around in mud, so they can get cool."

"I'm really glad to know that."

"I read about pigs when I was ten years old. They aren't really pigs, you know." The words rushed out, and I hardly knew what I was saying. Pigs weren't on my mind. That was frivolous . . . silly stuff, fun stuff to talk about. D.T. . . . my brother . . . my father . . . that was *real* stuff.

"What if something happens at the shop? What if my father can't come? You know how hard I had to work to persuade him to meet me here in the first place! He kept saying why didn't I just talk to him at home, the way I usually do."

"Dani, whoa! He'll be here, and if he isn't, you'll just set up another meeting. It has to happen, doesn't it?"

"I guess so," I said, uncertainly.

Laredo patted my arm. "It's a fairy tale, Dani. Long-lost brother returns to long-lost family."

I looked at my watch. "I should go in and get a booth."

"Call me later and tell me everything. I have to hear the next installment."

"Great. Now my life isn't a fairy tale, it's a soap opera."

Laredo kissed me on the cheek. "Ta, Dani, don't be nervous."

"Ta, Laredo." I held up crossed fingers. "Wish me luck."

"You mean wish D.T. luck, don't you?"

"I guess so." I stood with my hand on the door. "But me, too." Why not? It suddenly came over me. I had a brother. A real brother. Laredo was right. It *was* like a fairy tale.

Chapter 26

Dad came toward me, smiling and unwinding his green scarf. He kissed the top of my head and sat down and took off his ski jacket. "So what's the big secret? What's the important subject we had to come to Cosmo's to discuss?"

"You'll see." Was he going to act this way when D.T. got here? As if I were six and silly? "You want to order something?" I pushed the menu toward him.

"Your treat?"

"Certainly," I said.

Dad raised his hand to catch a waiter's attention. One of the men in black vests stopped at our booth. "Cup of coffee and an English muffin," Dad said. He rolled up his shirtsleeves. "You guys keep this place too warm. Turn down your thermostat."

The waiter looked at me. "I'll have a vanilla ice cream — " I began. Then I saw D.T. walking in, and my mouth closed on the word *soda*. The waiter went away, and D.T. came toward us.

The first thing I noticed was that his ankles were bare. Next, that his ponytail was gone! He'd cut his hair. And next, that he was wearing a tie. He stopped. "Hi, Dani."

Suddenly I didn't know what to do. Introduce him to Dad? Ask him to sit down? Where? Not next to Dad! Next to me? Somehow, that didn't seem right, either.

D.T. pulled his hands out of his pockets, then stuck them in again. "Hello, sir," he said to Dad.

"Hello . . ." Dad looked at me questioningly.

I wiped my hands on my jeans. "This is D.T. Goodman, Dad. D.T., my father — "

D.T. slid into the booth next to me. Dad didn't look just surprised: his eyebrows climbed straight up his forehead.

"Dad — " I wiped my hands down my jeans again. "What I asked you to come here about is about, uh, D.T. — "

"Dani," D.T. interrupted. "It's okay . . . let me do this."

"Do what?" my father said. "Are you looking for a job at the shop?" D.T. shook his head, but Dad went right on. "I'm always willing to help out young people; but you should probably talk to me at work." He reached into his pocket for a notebook. "If you want to set up an appointment — "

"Excuse me, excuse me, it has nothing to do

with a job," D.T. said nervously. He slid the zipper of his cardigan up and down. "Well . . . this is about you and me. I asked Dani to come here with me because she knows the whole thing. I thought it would make it easier . . . for everyone."

Dad had on what Lizbeth calls his "listening face."

D.T. took off his cardigan and pushed it down on the seat between us. As he did, his hand accidentally touched mine. It was ice cold. "Does my name mean anything to you?" he said.

"I don't think so," Dad said.

"Goodman." D.T. leaned across the table. "Donna Goodman? Does that — do you remember her?"

"Donna Goodman?" Dad repeated.

"Donna Goodman from Menands. Menands High School."

"I knew a Donna Goodman in high school," Dad said. A little color came up into his neck. "What's this all about?"

"She sends you her regards."

"How do you know her?"

"She's my mother."

"You're Donna's son?"

"Yes. I'm her son. Donna Goodman's son."

"That's quite a coincidence, you being friends with my daughter."

"We met — " I started, but D.T. interrupted.

"It isn't exactly a coincidence." His forehead was shining where he'd brushed his hair straight back. "I'm from California. Bakersfield. I came east in order to meet you. I just happened to meet Dani first."

"Wait a second. Back up," Dad said. "You came out here to meet me? Why?"

Just then the waiter came with our order, and we all stopped talking. "You want something?" Dad asked D.T.

He shook his head. As soon as the waiter left, he said, "Uh, my mother says you two were good friends."

Dad picked up his coffee cup, then put it down. "Three thousand miles is a pretty long trip just to meet an old friend of your mother's. Are you sure you're not looking for a job?"

"I'm working; I'm okay on that score." He pushed the ashtray around in front of him. "Do I look at all familiar to you?"

Dad studied D.T.'s face. "Well, I do think I see something of Donna around the nose and mouth. As I remember her, anyway. And I think you have her coloring. Maybe her hair, too. It's been a long time. I'm not sure how well my memory serves me."

"Twenty years," D.T. said. "My mother told me you two were in love."

Dad glanced at me. "It was high school. A lot of water under the bridge. I'm flattered she still remembers me."

"She's talked about you a lot."

"She was a terrific girl." Dad glanced at me again.

D.T. slid the ashtray one way, then the other, like a hockey puck. I could almost feel his tension

125

moving in waves, outward. "I came here, I crossed the country to see you because . . ." He pulled in a breath. The ashtray squeaked across the table. "I'm your son," he said.

I thought I was prepared to hear it — I'd heard it once already — but it shocked me. It was like a hit of ice water to the head. And it shocked Dad, too. I could see that. I could see it by the color that rushed into his face.

D.T. leaned back and closed his eyes. "There," he said, almost under his breath. "There. I did it."

"I don't have a son," Dad said. "What do you want? What is this, a joke, or something else?" His voice seemed hard to me, and I glanced at D.T. He had that hurt look on his face.

"It's not a joke, Dad." I was so tense my voice came out in a squeak.

"What do you have to do with this, Dani?"

"D.T. wouldn't joke about a thing like this. He's not that kind of person."

"I want to know what this is all about. Right now." Dad's voice had gone flat. The color kept seeping in and then out of his face.

"It's about me meeting my father," D.T. said. And he told Dad the things he'd told me — his mother's pregnancy, his grandparents taking her away . . .

Dad rolled his sleeves down, as if he were getting ready to leave. "I knew a Donna Goodman in high school, but I don't know anything about this," he said. "We broke up. I certainly never knew she was . . . I never knew anything about this. About you."

"I'm not saying you did. My mother told me the same thing."

"We were two kids. Donna was the one who wanted to break up. She was getting a lot of pressure from her family. That's right. That's the way it happened. One day she was gone." Dad snapped his fingers. "Just like *that*. She stopped coming to school. I found out she and her family had left the area."

"Did you try to find her, Dad?"

He didn't answer me. "Look, as far as I'm concerned," he said to D.T., "this is just a story." He pushed aside his cup. "I don't want to accuse you of anything, but what you're say-ing is serious, very serious."

"I know. It's also true."

"You can't just run around making accusations this way and expect people to believe you."

"Accusations? Mr. Merritt, I didn't come here to harass you. I came here to meet you. I had the thought . . . I guess it was dumb of me . . . that you'd want to meet me, too. That was my simple plan. Meet my father. Have my father meet me."

"That's a very nice speech, young man." Dad was half standing. "Very nice, but — "

"D.T. is my name. It stands for Daniel Thomas. Daniel for you, Thomas for my grand-father."

" — I mean to talk to your mother."

"She'll tell you what I just told you."

"Maybe she will. Even so — "

"Dad!" I said.

"Hush, Dani!" He was so upset he covered my mouth with his hand. Then he stood up. "Let's go, Dani."

D.T. wrote a number on a napkin. "That's our California phone." He wrote another number. The ink sank into the soft paper. "And that's mine at the Y, if you want to get in touch with me." He pushed the napkin toward Dad and left.

Chapter 27

"Want to go for a stroll, Dani? Dani . . ."

"Yes, Dad?"

"No, never mind. Let's wait a bit . . . let's wait until we're away from the house, then we'll talk."

"We're away now, Dad. Nobody can hear us."

"I thought you might like to know this, Dani. I called Donna Goodman today."

"D.T.'s mother."

"We talked about her son. I thought that she'd tell me it was all a fantasy of his, that the whole business was a concoction, a story . . . made up by a boy who wanted — "

"What, Dad? Wanted what?"

"I wasn't sure. When I thought over that hour we spent in Cosmo's, I realized the boy didn't have a father. That much was probably true. So

I asked myself, What did he want? Maybe a father figure in his life. Maybe some excitement, some lift, some thrill he wasn't getting out of his ordinary everyday life."

"Did D.T. seem like that to you?"

"You never know about people, Dani. You're still young, naive. People will surprise you. They'll show you one thing, then do another. I've seen bizarre things happen with people."

"D.T. isn't bizarre, Dad. He's a normal person. . . . What did his mother say?"

"Donna? Pretty much what he did."

"Did you . . . did you like talking to her?"

"I wouldn't put it that way. I didn't like it or dislike it. It was just something I had to do."

"What are you going to do now, Dad?"

"I don't know, Dani. I feel kind of stunned, I think. I've got to let this thing sink in."

"But you believe D.T. now, don't you?"

"I don't know. . . . I just don't know."

"Dad, you know what I just thought of? You didn't even have to call D.T.'s mother — "

"Shhh, Dani!"

"It's okay, Mom's upstairs. She can't hear us."

"Shut the door, anyway."

"Done. Okay? I just wanted to tell you this. All you had to do to find out if D.T. was telling the truth was look at the way he walks."

"The way he walks?"

"He walks just like you, Dad. Look, watch me, I'll show you. See? This is the way D.T. walks. One shoulder up, sort of leading with it.

And that's the way you walk, too."

"I do?"

"Dad, don't you know the way you walk?"

"I guess I'm finding out there might be a lot of things I don't know, Dani."

"Dani? How are you, Dani? I thought maybe you'd come over to the mall to visit me."

"I've been busy, D.T. I'm working almost every day after school with Greasepaint on the new production."

"You're painting?"

"No, no, it's the drama society. I work backstage. They're going to put on a musical in December, *Pump Boys and Dinettes*. It's really good."

"Anything new over your way?"

"My father talked to your mother."

"I know, she told me. She called me the other night."

"I think you just have to give him time, D.T."

"Time for what?"

"To sort of get used to the idea."

"He doesn't like the idea of having a son?"

"I don't think that's it, exactly."

"It's the way it looks from here, Dani."

"Dani, why don't horses like pizza?"

"Is this a quiz, Lizbeth?"

"No. I'm asking you something. Why don't horses like pizza? They like everything else people like. They like to eat. They like to work. They like to play. They like to sleep. They like to kiss. So why wouldn't they like pizza?"

"Okay, I bite. Why?"

"It's not a quiz, it's not a riddle. It's a *question*."

"Sorry, I don't know the answer."

"Stop laughing!"

"Who's laughing?"

"You are, Daddy's pet! I hate you. I wish I had another sister."

"How about a brother?"

"What?"

"Nothing, forget it. My mouth just slipped."

"Laredo? Hi! Your phone's been busy for hours."

"I was talking to Geo. That boy can talk!"

"He's cute, he's nice."

"I bet you're sorry I saw him first."

"Actually, *I* saw him first, Laredo. If you want to be literal about it."

"Are you still cranky because of feeling rejected by Jon?"

"I never even think about Jon Haberle."

"Come on, tell the truth."

"Well . . . I do stare every time I see him. Let's not talk about him. How's the big Geo romance going?"

"Good. In fact, great! We're doing it over the phone."

"You're doing *what* over the phone?"

"Don't get excited. Smooching. That's my mother's word for kissing. Isn't that a giggle?"

"You're kissing over the phone?"

"It's almost as good as the real thing. You ought to try it. Call Jon — "

"Don't be bizarre!"

"Use your imagination, Dani. Call him, pretend you're someone else and smooch him fast before he can get off."

"Okay, I'll call him and say I'm *you*."

"Dad, is it okay if Laredo knows about D.T.?"

"No, it's not okay."

"Oh. Well, Dad . . . uh . . . she knows."

"You told her? Why did you do that? Our business with D.T. is private, it's personal, it's *family business*, it's not for the consumption of the public."

"Laredo isn't the public, she's my best friend. Anyway, she thinks it's great that I have a brother."

"It's always easy for someone outside to comment. Dani, your mother doesn't even know."

"When are you going to tell her?"

"It's going to be a shock to her. She never even heard of Donna Goodman. Jody and I — well, you know what we say every anniversary. I was her first — "

" — very first love, and she was yours. That's what you both always say when you do your toast to each other."

"When I met your mother, the first time I saw her — "

"Dad, all the times I've heard you say that — talk about being each other's first loves —Dad — Dad. . . . It wasn't *true*."

"Yes, it was, Dani."

"What about D.T.'s mother? Donna Goodman?"

"That was different. We were so young. But
your mother — I don't know how to tell her
about this. I don't know what to do. I don't know
how she's going to react."

"Dani, can I come in?"

"Come in, Lizbeth. Come on, don't hang on
the door."

"I have a problem."

"Is it a horse problem? I don't think I can help
you with horse problems."

"This is a problem with you."

"Uh-oh. What is it?"

"You're always talking to Daddy these days!
Talk, talk, talk. You take a walk and talk. You
go in his study and talk. Talk, talk, talk. You go
in the backyard and talk."

"Lizbeth . . . it has nothing to do with you.
We're not talking about you."

"I don't care!"

"Lizbeth, I have things to talk over with Dad,
so — "

"*I have things to talk over with Daddy!*"

"Well, talk to him, then."

"He won't have time for me. He talks to you
always. Talk, talk, talk! No time for me! *That's
the problem.*"

"Dad . . . I've been thinking. Not telling Mom
anything about D.T. and his mom feels sort of
like lying to her, it feels bad to me."

"I'm not lying, Dani. I'm just not saying anything yet."

"You are going to tell her, though, aren't you?"

"In time. I need time."

"What about D.T.? It's been three weeks, Dad. He's waiting."

"Dani, please, keep your voice down. Your mother's in the next room."

"The door's shut."

"Nevertheless, keep it down."

"Okay . . . Is that better? Dad, don't you want a son?"

"What kind of question is that? It's not like going to the grocery store for a head of lettuce. I have you. I have Lizbeth. Did you ever hear me say I wanted sons instead of daughters? I love you two, I love you girls. I never wanted something else — "

"Dad, I didn't mean that you wanted a son instead of me or Lizbeth. Can't we just add D.T. to our family?"

"Dad, are you busy?"

"I am. Could you try not to call me at work unless it's really important?"

"I think this is important. Last night when we were talking, I forgot to tell you something. Lizbeth's feeling really jealous and upset. She's jealous of you and me. She says you're always talking to me. She feels like it's a big problem for her."

"Is that what she said?"

135

"She came right out with it. Dad, I think you should pay her some extra attention or something. Will you do it, Dad?"

"I will."

"Dad, will you definitely . . . you won't forget, will you?"

"Since when did I ever say I'd do something, Dani, and then not carry through?"

"Never before, Dad, but — "

"But what?"

"Well, lately — "

"Yes? Lately, *what?*"

"Lately, well, you know . . . It's like you not telling Mom — "

"All right, Dani, that's enough. I'll do that in my own good time."

"And Lizbeth?"

"What is this, an interrogation? Enough, Dani!"

Chapter 28

Saturday afternoon, Laredo and I were heading for the bus stop after spending the afternoon shopping, getting rid of the last of her money from working at Ice Dreams. It was too hot for the middle of October. Everyone was walking around in shirtsleeves and summer dresses.

I'd just pulled off my sweater when I saw a guy coming out the front door of the Y, wearing cutoffs and no shirt.

"Is that your brother?" Laredo said.

I squinched up my eyes to see better. She was right. D.T. was coming down the walk toward us. I started to wave, but all at once I didn't want him to see me — and I didn't want to see him. What could I say to him? *Sorry, D.T., sorry! I still don't have any good news to give you.*

He came toward us. "Dani!"

"Hi, D.T.," I said uncomfortably. "Not working today?"

He shook his head. "Hi, do I know you?" he said to Laredo.

She flashed her best smile. "I'm Laredo. My rude girlfriend forgot to introduce us. I know who you are, though. Remember when I came into Star to make a video for my little brother in Texas?"

"I remember." He rubbed his bare chest. "That was the first day Dani and I talked." He looked at our packages. "Let me guess. You girls have been shopping."

"You are *so* perceptive," Laredo flirted. "How is it living in the Y?"

"Not too homey; but it's just for a while. Did your brother like the video?"

Laredo nodded. "My stepmother made a video of him for me. I'm dying to see him in person. I may be going out there over Christmas vacation."

"You like your brother?" D.T. asked.

"I adore him," Laredo said. "Even though I've never met him."

D.T. laughed. "That's the way I feel about my little sister."

"Lizbeth," Laredo said, with a knowing look. "You've got a treat in store for you with her."

"She's riding today," I said. "She and her girlfriend are both at the stables."

"She's a super rider," Laredo boasted, as if Lizbeth were her sister. "You ought to see her in her riding getup, on that big horse, D.T. She's smashing."

"At least I won't have to go all the way to Texas to meet her. Right, Dani? Just the other side of town." He was looking at me hopefully.

"I wish I could tell you something," I mumbled.

"Everything's still the same, then?" he said. "Nothing's happening?"

"Well . . . Dad's thinking about things." I remembered Dad saying *In my own good time.* . . . When was that going to be?

The bus was coming then, and we had to go. I was glad. We said good-bye and crossed the street. "D.T.'s really nice," Laredo said as we sat down in back.

"I know."

"Isn't it amazing to get a brother — just like *that*? Isn't it like getting a present you never expected?"

"I still really don't know him. I've only talked to him a few times."

"If he was my brother, I'd talk to him every day!"

"I can't . . . because of my mother."

"When is your father going to tell her? How long is he going to wait?"

"I don't know! Drop the subject, please." It made me uncomfortable to criticize my father. It made me uncomfortable to think I knew something my mother didn't. And it made me really uncomfortable to think of D.T. waiting . . . and waiting. . . .

When we walked into the house, the phone was ringing. "I bet it's Mom," I said, "checking up on me. I told her I'd be home an hour ago."

I picked up the receiver. "Dani?" my mother said. "I've been calling and calling."

"Mom, sorry. We took longer than we thought —"

"Never mind that," she said. "Something's happened. Lizbeth didn't come back from her trail ride."

Chapter 29

The headline in the next day's paper read, TWO GIRLS LOST IN FOREST. The story was on the front page of the Sunday paper.

The entire sheriff's department and dozens of volunteers tramped the woods with searchlights for hours Saturday night looking for Lizbeth Merritt and Kirstie Vandaam, two young girls who became lost in Meimberg Memorial Forest while horseback riding earlier that day.

Sheriff Lynell G. Packwood said that over the years, numerous people have been lost in the forest. In 1979, Will R. Glover, a forty-nine-year-old man, died of exposure after only two days in the forest.

Sheriff Packwood directed the search for the girls from the home of Leila Sandler-Frost, the owner of Our Horse Farm, where the two girls often rent horses for trail rides. Besides volunteer searchers, Sheriff Packwood had the services of the city police department helicopter, which is equipped with a high-intensity searchlight and a trained crew.

Searchers included Lizbeth Merritt's parents and her sister, Danita Merritt. At ten minutes past one o'clock in the morning, close to the point when the sheriff was considering calling off the search for the night, shouts from the direction of the forest were heard by people holding vigil at the stable. Moments later, one of the search parties emerged with the girls.

A cheer went up from the waiting crowd. Though both girls said they were "starved," they appeared alert and cheerful as they were reunited with their families. Lizbeth and Kirstie are both accomplished horsewomen, according to Mrs. Sandler-Frost, and have ridden often on the well-marked trails in the forest with no problems. "We took a wrong turn," said Kirstie Vandaam, "and lost the way."

As dusk fell, the girls said, they dismounted and tried to let their horses lead them out. "Then it got dark, and we suddenly lost each other," said Lizbeth Merritt.

"That was the scariest time, when I didn't know where Kirstie was."

After that, the girls decided to stay in one place. Once, they saw the helicopter going over. "We screamed and waved," Kirstie reported. "We saw the white light going away. I cried. I thought everybody thought we were dead and they wouldn't look for us anymore. But Lizbeth said we just had to wait."

And wait they did until they heard voices. Lizbeth Merritt called, "Hello, who are you?" She went on to explain, "When they said they were looking for us, we ran up and hugged everybody."

The newspaper carried pictures of Kirstie in her mom's arms and Lizbeth being hugged by Mom and Dad. There was a third picture, too, captioned, "Lizbeth Merritt's two sisters celebrate her safe return." It was a picture of Laredo and me, Laredo with her hair waving in the breeze, and me with my glasses on crooked.

"Laredo's not my sister," Lizbeth said. "They made a mistake in my story. Mommy, I'm calling them up and telling them."

"Are you?" Mom laughed. "Don't worry about it. You're here with us, that's what matters."

"Anyway, Laredo's sort of like a sister to you," I said. "A half sister or a quarter sister." I looked

143

at Dad. "It would be fun having another sib, wouldn't it, Lizbeth?"

"Maybe," she said, cuddling with Dad. She got all the attention she could have wanted from him that day. He couldn't stop hugging her and saying, "My baby. You're safe now, my baby."

The first few times, I chimed right in. "You did great, Lizbeth. I'm proud of you." But then, when Dad kept saying, "My baby," to her, I thought, *Okay, Dad, enough!* And I wondered why he wasn't thinking of another "baby" in his life that he didn't fuss over *at all*. Or, rather, another "baby" *not* in his life. D.T., of course. He was my father's first baby, wasn't he?

We all stayed home Monday, like it was a holiday. It *was* a holiday. No school for Lizbeth and me. No work for Mom and Dad. Mom said we all deserved a day off. We sat around the house, eating and reading and playing Monopoly, Lizbeth's favorite game . . . *and* answering the phone.

The phone had been ringing off the hook for her on Sunday, and it went on ringing on Monday. She must have told her story a dozen times, and each time Dad's eyes reddened and got teary.

The phone rang. "Oooh, again?" Lizbeth sighed, but she bounced up. "Hello, this is Lizbeth Merritt speaking. . . . Who? Oh! Mrs. Damson!" She turned and kind of glowed at us. It was her principal.

144

". . . so *then* Kirstie and I said to each other we should stay in one place," she said in her high, little-girl's voice. "Because I had read this book about somebody being lost and how they went in circles and got really lost and got sick and everything from no water or food."

Dad's eyes teared. "When I think of what could have happened to her," he said to my mother, "I feel actually sick. Did I tell you, Jody, that I dreamed about it last night?"

Mom leaned her chin in her hand. She could be brisk or sharp sometimes if you annoyed her. She could be that way with Dad, too, but leaning there, she looked like, well, a girl in love. And I remembered what Dad had said. *She was my first true love and I was hers.*

"It was one of those dreams where you can't believe it didn't happen. I had to get out of bed and check on Lizzie right away."

"She's okay," Mom said, looking over at Lizbeth, who was still talking on the phone. "She seems to have taken the whole thing really well."

"I know. But it could so easily have been different."

"Dad, it wasn't. Nothing bad happened," I said.

"But it could have. That's what hurts me. That's what scares me, the idea that we so nearly lost her."

"We didn't nearly lose her, Dad! Lizbeth kept her head, and we found her. She's right here, and like Mom says, she's okay."

"People have been lost in that forest and never come out, Dani."

"Dad," I said, jumping up. "You're so upset about Lizbeth, but what about D.T.?" I heard the words coming out of my mouth, and I couldn't stop them. "What about *him*, Dad? How about getting upset about him?"

Chapter 30

"Who's D.T.?" Mom said.

Dad was looking at me as if I'd betrayed him.

"Dad, I'm sorry — " I stopped myself. Was I sorry? I wanted the truth out. I wanted Mom to know. I wanted things settled!

"Who's D.T.?" Mom said again.

Lizbeth was still talking on the phone. Dad was folding and refolding the newspaper. He looked at me for a long time. Then he glanced over at Lizbeth. Then at me again.

"I just don't know how to say this," he said to Mom. "I've been trying to find the right way to say it."

Mom watched him attentively.

"But I guess there is no right way. Remember when we met?"

"Of course I remember."

"Remember how we said to each other we'd never loved anyone else?" Dad was sitting on the couch with one leg drawn up under the other, like the number four. "Well, it was true for me, but not completely. There was a girl in high school . . . we were in love. Three weeks ago, I found out . . . I met her son." He paused. "He's my son."

"Say that again," Mom said.

"I found out I had a son."

"You found out — " Mom glanced at me.

"Dani knows about it," Dad said.

"Why?" Mom said. "Who was this girl? What was your relationship to her?"

"It was high school stuff. We were in love . . . we thought so . . . and then we broke up."

"She didn't tell you she was pregnant?"

Dad shook his head. "Nothing."

"She didn't tell you after the baby was born?"

He shook his head again.

"You must have heard something. Menands is not that big a place, Daniel!"

"She moved. She and her parents. They left. They went to California. That's where he was born. One day Donna was in school, the next, gone. The whole family was gone."

"Didn't you think it was a little strange? Didn't you have the least little suspicion?"

"No. I told you, we'd broken up. She'd broken up with me a month, maybe six weeks, earlier. I didn't connect it."

"And now, after all these years, this boy pops up and says he's your son? How do you know this is true? And what's Dani got to do with all this? When did all this happen?"

"I met the boy a month ago."

"You've known about this for *a month*? And I'm just hearing it now?"

"Jody, it's a long, complicated story."

"I'm sure it is. Nevertheless — "

"It's been hard for me. I literally did not know how to tell you about this."

"Why? Why was that so hard?"

"I was worried," Dad said. "I didn't know how you'd take it. It's always been you and me. Maybe I was trying for damage control by putting it off."

"Really?" Mom's voice was cool. "I don't think you succeeded, Daniel." She got up and walked out of the room.

"Jody!" Dad said.

"Mommy," Lizbeth said, hanging up the phone. "Where're you going?"

"A movie," Mom yelled. "I'm going to a movie. By myself!"

"Without us?" Lizbeth said. "Mommy, that's not fair."

"Shut up, Lizbeth, you're always thinking of yourself," I said. I heard the back door slam. Then a minute later, I heard one of the cars driving off.

Chapter 31

Mom wasn't back by suppertime. I made pizza for us. Well, I took it out of the freezer and put it in the oven, anyway.

"You girls are going to go to school tomorrow," Dad said, while we were fixing the salad.

"Are you going to work?" Lizbeth asked.

We sat down to eat. Usually Dad liked to talk at supper, but he didn't say much that night.

Lizbeth was tired and got whiney. "I wish Mommy was here." She leaned on her elbow.

"Elbows off the table, this is not a stable," I said.

"Be quiet, Dani." She looked like she was going to cry.

Dad and I cleaned up the kitchen together. "Are you going to tell Lizbeth about D.T.?" I asked.

Dad put down the plate he was rinsing. He looked surprised, as if he hadn't thought of it until just then. "Finish up here, Dani." I heard him go upstairs.

Later, I went into Lizbeth's room and sat on the edge of her bed. "You want to talk about anything?" She was lying on her back with the covers up to her chin, reading *Black Beauty* for about the sixth time.

"Talk about what?" she said.

"Anything. Whatever. Daddy came to talk to you, didn't he?"

She put down her book. "He told me about my half brother. What if I don't like having a half brother, Dani?"

"He's nice, Lizbeth."

"Why do you know him and I don't?" she complained. "That's not fair."

I told her how I'd met D.T. in You Can Be a Star, Too. "When Laredo made a video for her little brother. D.T. was working there."

"Laredo doesn't have a brother," Lizbeth said.

"Yes, she does. He's a half brother, too. He lives in Texas. He's two years old."

"How old is my half brother?"

"Nineteen."

"Old!" Lizbeth sat up, smiling. "I thought . . . I thought he was younger."

"No, he's nineteen. He was born a long time before you and me."

She giggled with embarrassment. "I got mixed up from what Daddy said. I thought D.T. was going to be the youngest one."

151

"And you were afraid you wouldn't be the baby of the family anymore?"

Lizbeth nodded sheepishly. She was wearing her horse pajamas, with her hair all loose and frizzy from being taken out of braids. I gave her a little squeeze. "Don't worry, Lizzie, you'll always be the baby of the family. Unless Mom has another baby," I added.

"What?" she said. "Is she going to do that?"

"Lizbeth, I was just joking. Relax."

The next morning, going down the stairs, I could hear Mom and Dad in the kitchen, talking. She hadn't come back until late last night. "All I can say is, you should have told me right away," Mom was saying. "No matter how you felt, you should have trusted me to understand."

"And I still think I was right to be worried about you. You were pretty shocked and upset yesterday, Jody."

"I admit it. I had to get used to the idea. But I didn't jump over a cliff, did I?"

"Taking off in the car — "

"Come on, I told you where I was going. I just sat in a movie for six hours."

"Was it any good?" Dad said.

"No!" Mom said. "Listen, Daniel, I want to tell you something. You didn't just let me down. You let that boy down, too. Do you know how long a month is to a kid? An eternity."

"Jody, another thing. He's a stranger to us, even if he is my — "

I hesitated outside the kitchen. Was their conversation private? Should I interrupt it? I'd never

152

hesitated in my life before to walk into any room in our house. Then I thought of D.T., wondered where he was right now. Eating breakfast alone at a counter in a doughnut shop? That made me feel sad for him.

Mom saw me. "Come in, Dani, breakfast is ready."

I sat down at the table. "Good morning."

"Good morning, sweetie," Mom said and went right on talking to Dad. "Maybe he is a stranger, but he's a child, first."

"A child? He's nineteen."

"That's still a boy," Mom said. "You should know that."

I wondered if D.T. would like it that my parents — his father, his stepmother — were talking about him. I thought it would make him laugh to hear Mom call him a child. And then I thought of something else. For once my parents had both forgotten the morning inspection, forgotten to look me over to see if I'd survived the horrors and rigors of sleeping through the night in my own bed. Oh, joy!

Chapter 32

D.T. came to the house a few days later for supper. We were all waiting, all a little nervous, I think. When the bell rang, I said, "I'll get it."

"I'll get it!" Lizbeth said.

"Girls," Mom said, "let your father do it."

But then we all went to the door, crowding together. D.T. looked startled to see all of us there. "Hi, D.T.," I said. Almost automatically I looked down at his feet. Sneakers. No socks.

"D.T.," Dad said. He held out his hand and they shook.

Mom hugged him. "I'm Jody Merritt, Dani's mother." She patted his back. "We're so glad you're here."

"I'm your sister," Lizbeth said. "Did you read about me in the newspaper?"

In the living room, we all sat down. It was

quiet for a moment. We were looking at D.T., and he was looking at us. I saw him glance at the pictures of me and Lizbeth on top of the TV.

"I think you have the same nose as Grandma Merritt," Mom said. "That same little nose."

"My mother says I look like her father," D.T. said.

Mom brought out the photo album and we all clustered around, looking at the family pictures. That helped break the ice.

"Where do they live?" D.T. asked, pointing to a picture of Grandpa and Grandma Merritt. "Do they still live around here?"

"Your grandmother lives in Florida," Dad said. "Your grandfather died three years ago."

"What was he like?"

"Well . . . a nice man."

"Very nice," Mom said firmly. "Generous person. People liked him a lot. You would have liked him, D.T."

"I'd like to visit her . . . Grandma Merritt," he said.

"I don't know if that's a good idea," Dad said. "She doesn't know about you . . . it might be too much of a shock. She's not that young, and she was never very flexible."

D.T. got kind of quiet after that. I wondered if he was upset. Did he think Dad didn't want him to know the rest of our family? It was D.T.'s family, too, now. We all were. I knew that, but I still had to keep reminding myself.

I'd been calling him brother and being really enthusiastic about him, but it wasn't like saying,

155

"Lizzie's my sister." I knew *that* right in my bones, or my heart, or my stomach. Whatever. It was down there inside me. It was the way it was, and it didn't matter how irritated I got with Lizbeth, it was still the way it was and always would be. She was my sister. Period. End of discussion.

But with D.T. I had to keep telling myself — *he's my brother*. It was like learning something new, having to repeat it, the way you practice when you're trying to remember the answers for an important quiz. *D.T.'s my brother . . . D.T.'s my brother . . .* All through supper, I found myself thinking that.

Maybe Lizzie was, too. A couple times I caught her suddenly looking across the table at D.T. with her mouth open. And was Dad saying it to himself in his own way? *D.T.'s my son . . . D.T.'s my son . . .* I knew he believed it now, but how did he *feel* about it? Amazed? Happy? Confused? And what about Mom? In a way, she was acting the most natural of all of us, maybe *because* she wasn't related to D.T.

"What do your parents do, D.T.?" she asked.

"When I started grade school, my mother started college. It took her eight years to get her degree. Now she's an editor on a trade newspaper. My stepfather's a policeman."

"Donna's an editor?" Dad said. "I didn't know she was that smart."

"Dad!" I said.

"Well . . . I guess she's changed."

"My mother was always smart," D.T. said,

maybe a little stiffly. "Maybe you just couldn't see it, Daniel." That's what he and my father had agreed D.T. would call him for now.

"Maybe you didn't expect to see it, Dan," my mother said.

"Maybe," Dad agreed. "Times were different then."

"More sexist," I said.

"That was one of the things my grandparents didn't like about you," D.T. said to Dad. "They thought you were sidetracking her. They knew my mother was smart. They didn't want her to miss out on her education. And they didn't think you had any ambition. Sorry. I don't mean to be rude. I guess you knew all that."

"I knew Donna's father didn't like me," Dad admitted. "But he was wrong. I had ambition, I just didn't have a grasp on what I wanted to do."

D.T. brought out pictures of his mother, stepfather, and grandparents. Lizbeth got confused. "Are they my grandparents, too?" She finally got it straight. D.T. was really patient, explaining that one set of his grandparents were hers, but one set wasn't. And vice versa.

"And what are you going to do now?" Dad said.

"About what?"

"Well . . . work. School. You're not going to go on clerking in that video store for the rest of your life, are you?"

D.T. put his fork down. "Actually, I've been thinking about going home. I've done what I came for here. I miss my mother."

"I bet you do," Mom said. She got up and brought in the dessert. Strawberry shortcake.

D.T.'s eyes lit up. "My favorite."

"So, you get the biggest piece," Mom said.

"It's my favorite, too," Lizbeth said quickly.

We all laughed.

Around nine o'clock, we got into the car and drove D.T. to the Y. Lizbeth, D.T., and I were in the backseat. "Are you mad at me?" I asked D.T., suddenly.

"Should I be?"

"I'm afraid. . . . I don't think I was nice tonight. . . . I mean, we didn't really talk."

He laughed. "My worrywart sister."

When Dad pulled up in front of the Y, he turned around and shook hands with D.T. again. It was so awkward and formal. And then everyone started being exceptionally polite. D.T. thanked my mother for the meal. She thanked him for coming. Dad said, "Well, good night, then. Keep in touch." And D.T. got out of the car.

I had this sort of quaking in my stomach. I didn't know what it was — fear, I think. I watched D.T. walk up the steps. Dad started to pull away from the curb. Suddenly I said, "Stop! Let me out. Dad!" I had the door open. I jumped out before Dad even stopped.

I ran into the Y. D.T. was in the lobby, sliding quarters into a soda machine. "D.T.!" I didn't have any idea what I was doing, why I'd come running in that way. I only knew that I had to see him again for a moment — say *something* . . .

"What's up, Dani?" A can of soda bumped down.

"I have to — to tell you something."

"What's that?"

"I don't know. . . ."

He was staring at me. "You have to tell me something, but you don't know what it is?"

I nodded. And then I did know. "D.T. I'm so glad you're my brother."

Chapter 33

D.T. decided to stay around for a couple more weeks. That was in October. In November, after Mom said she wanted him here for Thanksgiving, he added a few more weeks, but he said he was definitely going back to California for Christmas. Then it turned out his mom and stepfather were going to Hawaii over the holidays, so he stayed through December, too.

After that, I told him he couldn't leave until after my birthday, which was the third week in January. By that time, my parents had asked him to move in with us. My father was going to clear out his study downstairs and make it into a bedroom for D.T.

"No need," D.T. said. "I'm on my way back home any day now."

"You're living on one foot," Dad said. "You're

always on your way out any day, any moment."

"I can't stay here forever," D.T. said.

"I'd like to find a place for you in the print shop," Dad said. "You're too smart for the job you're doing."

"I've got plans about college. I'll be going back. Maybe next semester."

"Well, you know, anything I can do to help you . . ."

"I know. Thanks. I appreciate it."

Dad and D.T. were nice together, almost *too* nice, *too* careful. I talked to Laredo about it, and we decided the difference between the way we were with our parents and the way D.T. was with Dad was this: *We* knew, no matter what we did or said or thought, our parents wouldn't stop being our parents, and we wouldn't stop being their kids. But D.T. didn't have that belief built into him about Dad.

I don't remember why D.T. stayed through February, but I know about March. I got him to agree to stay until his birthday, which was, in a weird coincidence, only three days before Mom and Dad's anniversary. He was going to be twenty. They were going to be married seventeen years.

We made a big party in the house: tons of food and all of us dressed up. I wore a long skirt, dangley earrings, one of Mom's silk blouses, and I pulled my hair over to one side. Lizzie had a long skirt, too, but she sort of ruined the total effect by wearing her white blouse printed all over with blue horses. D.T. showed up in a black jacket, black-and-white-striped tie, a thin black ribbon to tie back his ponytail (which he'd grown again), and a white carnation in his lapel.

I whistled at him. Then I looked down. Still no socks.

A lot of my parents' friends, and people they worked with, and our neighbors came to the party. Dad was introducing D.T. to everyone. "This is my son, D.T. Goodman."

Laredo was taking pictures with a camera her father had sent her instead of plane tickets for Christmas. She showed me the latest picture of her brother, Jasper. A little freckled boy in a white shirt and red bow tie. She kissed the picture. "Maybe this summer," she said.

Mom asked Laredo to take a picture of our whole family. We started lining up. "Dani, get next to your mother," Laredo said. She had the camera to her eye. "When I say 'dirty socks,' you guys smile."

"Where's D.T.?" I said. "D.T., we need you here."

"I'm camera shy."

"No, you're not. You get over here," I said. D.T. came and stood behind me.

"You guys ready yet?" Laredo said.

"No," Dad said. "D.T." He crooked his finger. "Come over here next to me." He reached over and got his arm around D.T.

Laredo said, "Dirty socks." We all smiled. The flashcube went off.

Mom framed the picture for the top of the TV.

162

I'm a little blurred in it, because my head was swiveling around to look at D.T. and Dad. Mom and Lizbeth look fine, they're smiling. And Dad is hugging D.T., who is leaning in toward him with this strange expression on his face, like he wants to laugh and cry at the same time.

I guess that's the end of the story.

Well, not actually. Stories like this — I mean, stories of our real life — never end, do they? How could they? That would be unreal life. So I'll just say this much more.

My parents still hover quite a lot (I guess old habits are hard to break), but they definitely don't do it as much as they used to.

D.T. went back to California in May. We might not see him for a while. He's going to go back to college in the fall. Dad calls him about once a month to talk. Whenever he gets off the phone he says he's really getting on with D.T. now. "My son and I have a good relationship going," he says.

I've been writing to D.T. I like to write letters. He writes postcards back. Four or five words seem to be his limit. One went like this, "Hey, Dani! Miss you. Love, D.T." I thought that was pretty nice. It would be even nicer to get a real long letter, but that's okay. I have plenty of time to get letters from D.T. — the rest of my life.

And meanwhile, anytime I want to, I can sit down and start a letter with the words, "Dear Brother . . ."

About the Author

NORMA FOX MAZER is the author of more than twenty books for young readers, among them the Newbery honor winner *After the Rain*, as well as *Taking Terri Mueller*, *When We First Met*, and *Downtown*. Ms. Mazer has twice won the Lewis Carroll Shelf Award; she has also won the California Young Reader Medal and has been nominated for the National Book Award.

D, My Name Is Danita is a companion book to *A, My Name Is Ami*; *B, My Name Is Bunny*; *C, My Name Is Cal*; and *E, My Name Is Emily*, all published by Scholastic.

Ms. Mazer lives with her husband, author Harry Mazer, in the Pompey Hills outside Syracuse, New York.

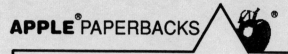

APPLE® PAPERBACKS

Pick an Apple and Polish Off Some Great Reading!

BEST-SELLING APPLE TITLES

❑ MT43944-8 **Afternoon of the Elves** Janet Taylor Lisle — $2.75

❑ MT43109-9 **Boys Are Yucko** Anna Grossnickle Hines — $2.95

❑ MT43473-X **The Broccoli Tapes** Jan Slepian — $2.95

❑ MT40961-1 **Chocolate Covered Ants** Stephen Manes — $2.95

❑ MT45436-6 **Cousins** Virginia Hamilton — $2.95

❑ MT44036-5 **George Washington's Socks** Elvira Woodruff — $2.95

❑ MT45244-4 **Ghost Cadet** Elaine Marie Alphin — $2.95

❑ MT44351-8 **Help! I'm a Prisoner in the Library** Eth Clifford — $2.95

❑ MT43618-X **Me and Katie (The Pest)** Ann M. Martin — $2.95

❑ MT43030-0 **Shoebag** Mary James — $2.95

❑ MT46075-7 **Sixth Grade Secrets** Louis Sachar — $2.95

❑ MT42882-9 **Sixth Grade Sleepover** Eve Bunting — $2.95

❑ MT41732-0 **Too Many Murphys** Colleen O'Shaughnessy McKenna — $2.95